THE LONE PINE RANCH

Drexel Calhoun had quit a good job as top hand with Paul Bowman to sign up as foreman of the Lone Pine Ranch. But when he found the Lone Pine was owned by a woman he was ready to give up the whole shebang. It was only the challenge of the enemies his new boss was fighting that kept him on; that and a desire to know who had perforated the hombre on the stagecoach who looked so much like himself.

The most powerful ranchers in the region, led by Abelard Vick of the Wagon Wheel, were gunning for the Lone Pine. And besides having a woman owner, the Pine was handicapped by a small and untrustworthy crew.

The Lone Pine Ranch

The
Lone Pine Ranch

by

LYNN WESTLAND

WILDSIDE PRESS

1

Calhoun left the stage at The Corners. He had
paid his fare straight through to Sage, and it had
been his intention to ride all the way, but now impatience stirred too strongly in him. Two days of
creaking, jolting discomfort, with the hot dust
sifting up through the floor boards and the taste
of alkali in his mouth; of being crowded among
a load of sweaty humanity and badgered with talk
by a garrulous female who seemed to find something romantic in the tall, lithe leanness of him
was enough.

He was, he confessed to himself, an impatient

man. When things did not go to his liking, it had always been his custom to make a change. Either a man could correct things, or he could get away to a new country and a new job. *A man was a fool to do things he didn't want to do, to take things he didn't like. To be pushed around.*

That was his philosophy. And so, hating the crowded, comfortless stage, he emptied his pockets of half the money he owned and bought a good horse, a hammer-headed roan, long in the barrel, deep-chested, with a rolling cold eye like his own. The cayuse might be ornery, but it would have stamina. A saddle took most of the rest. If you wanted independence, you stayed poor. But what more could a man ask for than a good horse and a saddle and the right to do as he pleased?

Thereafter he followed not far behind the stage. It was hot, with an untempered sun in a brassy sky, and his big roan churned the endless dust. But the air held its old breath of freedom. Drexel Calhoun did not regret the depletion of his pocket-book. Especially with a good job waiting, ahead.

Eyes half closed against the endless rolling flatness of a land burnt dust-brown under the sun, unrelieved as far as eye could reach save for occasional whitish strips of alkali and the distant blue outline of hills, he found himself thinking a little

8

wistfully of the name of the ranch. Lone Pine Ranch. It had a poetic sound at which he had snorted disdainfully when first hearing it. Calhoun had no time for poets or dreamers. But now he liked the sound of it, tried to visualize it.

There was remoteness and coolness in the name. It ought to be a mountain-girt land of plashy streams and broad green meadows, though the country, so far, held little promise of anything like that. A more desolate country he'd never seen.

But by mid-afternoon it was beginning to change. Here were low foothills, and the occasional coulees which gashed their slopes had brush cradled in their hollows—clumps of thorn-apple, blankets of rose briars spread like a thorny mat. Now and then choke-cherry or service-berry, sometimes a clump of currant or the sharp clear red of dogwood. There were juniper clinging to the hills, stunted and gray-green from dust and heat, and once the clear whiteness in a coulee's depths of aspen, a handful of them standing bravely against the rim of the prairie.

Here an occasional cabin, nearly all of them long deserted, began to show. Paintless, desolate monuments to men who had come hopefully and tried to make a living, had failed and moved on—or died and been done with hopeless trying. *Fools,* Calhoun thought briefly, in a land such as this.

Boarded up windows, doors forced ajar by the curious and left to stand sagging on a yawning emptiness, were all that was left. Viewing the country with an experienced eye, Calhoun guessed that cattlemen would range stock here in spring, and perhaps again after the fall rains had started, but that no one would try to live in the land in the summer.

No one not compelled to, or having good sense. He had passed four change houses, stage stops, during the day, with caretakers twisted and warped like their environment, men who looked at him with remote surprise, a little wistfully, with the faint flowering of hope that he might linger to chat a while. Twice he had done so, squatting in the shade, drinking tepid, brackish water, allowing his horse a breather.

He had seen no one else all day. No wagons, no men on horseback. The stage was ahead of him, and that was all. There were no farms, no ranches in that vast stretch of hot bleakness.

It was mid-afternoon when he rounded one of the first bends to appear in the road, made by the sprawling foothills here, and saw another horseman, a quarter of a mile ahead. A long coulee ran back from the road, making almost a valley. There was still a trace of greenness down its length, as though a spring had started strongly and flowed that far most of the summer, before giving up the unequal struggle in a land and air too thirsty for the living.

Farther up, where the spring must have had its beginning, the coulee widened to a little meadow, two or three trees, and there was an old house, deserted-looking like the others. Calhoun saw with narrowing gaze that it was built of logs, and bigger, more substantial than any of the others which he had passed during the day. Those were cottonwood trees, and that seemed to mark the real transition from prairie to foothills.

The other horseman dipped out from the shelter of the coulee onto the road, and it was that which caused the sudden appearance as if from nowhere. Evidently he'd been up there by that old house, Calhoun decided. And he was just in time to see the thing happen, while still too far distant to be able to do anything about it.

The jogging cayuse ahead, which had been trotting with drooping head and a despondent air of weariness, was suddenly galvanized to a wild frenzy. It went into the air with a wild twisting, sunfishing plunge, as though red-hot coals had scorched its hoofs. It came down in a thrashing terror that sent it sliding, sprawling. And then, a moment later, it had struggled wildly up again and was running madly away from there. But not before that twisting gyration had unseated its rider.

He was stretched full length on the ground, there in the road. Lying as though dazed. Calhoun stared, and swore, and touched his own tiring horse with the spurs, and the big hammer-head confirmed his judgment with a burst of speed.

Riding up, Calhoun confirmed what had amazed him at the start. This rider wore overalls and a big hat, which had fallen off. The sun glinted on long hair turned gold under its rays, and there was no mistake now. This was a woman, and young. Not over seventeen or eighteen, with a pretty, rather sullen face under that heavy golden hair. There was a smudge of dirt across one cheek, and terror in her now wide open eyes.

She was struggling to sit up, there in the dust, as Calhoun neared, and there was still a half dazed look on her face, which confirmed his first guess, that she had been thrown hard, knocked half unconscious for the first few moments. She wore a gunbelt and holster like any cowboy, and silver-mounted spurs. But the holster was empty now, and he caught the gleam of sun along the gun-barrel, a dozen feet away, further testimony to the force with which she had been thrown from the saddle.

Calhoun observed that she was not looking at him, that she was not even aware of his approach. There was horror and a choking sort of terror in her eyes, and the reason was only too clear. A big rattlesnake, thick as Calhoun's arm, was coiled before her, not a yard away. The girl was staring with repugnant fascination as its tail made a chilling crescendo of sound and the flat, ugly head waved back and forth.

Calhoun's own revolver was in holster. He had never made a faster draw or a better shot. The head was almost severed from the swelling neck beneath, the coils sprang suddenly into wildly thrashing convulsion. And as he left the saddle, fearing that she would faint, intending to drag her back, he saw a second reptile, suddenly in coil, only a dozen feet away.

The girl screamed at the shot, as though a thralldom in her throat had been released at the sound. Calhoun, on his feet now, shot the second rattler with a cool sureness equal to that of his first bullet. By then, the girl was on her feet, staring at him, and clutching at her pant's leg with one hand, terror still in her face.

He saw it then—the fang marks on her left

13

ankle, in the fleshy part of the leg. Two tiny, evil-looking punctures, around which discoloration was already beginning to show. She wore a low, well-cut riding boot, and socks like a man, and there had been nothing to protect the bare flesh from the strike of the snake. Seeing it, understanding of what had happened came to him.

She had been riding, pensive, thoughtful, when he had first seen her. And her cayuse had apparently been between the two rattlers before it had sensed their presence. Both had undoubtedly given warning at once, and the double crescendo of blood-chilling sound, the bitter-fetid scent of snake had all come to it together, and had thrown the horse into that wild frenzy. In attempting to jump and avoid one it had almost come on top of the other, had tried again to twist in the air, and that had sent it sprawling, its wild gyrations flinging the girl out of the saddle.

And probably almost on one of the rattlers. It had struck—and the girl, dazed by her fall, had not moved at first, which had probably saved her from a repeated attack. But when she had started to revive and begun to stir, the aroused reptile had been full of fight again. Calhoun had seen plenty of them that way, half blind, ugly, at this season of the year.

"Sit down," he said, and there was kindness and reassurance in his voice. "They're dead now. Let me look at that leg."

The girl stared at him a moment, her eyes big with pain and the nightmare of the last few moments, but some of the terror faded out as she understood. There was something reassuring about this man, the way he had materialized in her moment of need, and the coldly efficient manner in which he had dispatched the rattlers.

Even in that moment, she noted that he was perhaps seven or eight years her senior, that he had a tanned, efficient look about him, coupled with a sharp, arrogant pride. He had heavy black hair, a smooth-shaven face, black eyes to match. He was handsome in a reckless sort of way.

She sank down limply, her knees seemingly of jelly. Instantly, with no word of apology, Calhoun was on one knee beside her, swiftly rolling back the overalls. Otherwise her outfit was an expensive one, like the hand-made boots and the silver-mounted spurs.

He was on his feet again, a knife in his hand. He opened the blade, slashed off one of his saddle thongs and, dropping down beside her, tied it just above her knee and, using the knife for leverage, twisted it until the cord sank into her flesh and her

15

face went white. He made it fast with the lace from her boot, ripping it expertly out, pulling the boot off.

Then he studied the punctures again, hesitating with the knife-blade, and she knew that he was thinking of slashing the wound open, and steadied herself for the ordeal. Instead, he stooped, and she felt his mouth at the wound, and for a long moment he sucked hard, then spat out the poison and repeated the process twice more, his lips creating so strong a vacuum that she could feel it.

"How close is the next town?" he asked then, still holding the knife, and thought bleakly of the long day during which he had passed through no towns at all.

"A couple of miles—to Sage," she answered, and now her voice was steady.

"That's luck," he said. "Would there be more of it, so that we could, by any chance, find a doctor there?"

"Doc Fenton's there," she said. "If he's in town. He most generally is."

"Then we've done enough till we can get to him," Calhoun said, relief in his voice. He pocketed the knife and stood up. "We'll be there in a hurry."

He picked her up as if she had been a child, and she was conscious of his strength as he swung her

16

into the saddle, then jumped up behind her. The hammer-head was inclined to resent the double burden and be fractious about it, but Calhoun quickly cured that. He was in no mood for foolishness.

He rode hard, despite the long miles behind. He was a little surprised and considerably pleased at the time he had already made. He had figured that Sage would be at least another five miles beyond.

They climbed a little, came to the crest of the slope, and a low valley opened out abruptly below them. There was Sage, at the foot of the slope, with one long street, and a clustering crowd in the middle of it. A man with a black bag was just getting back to his feet, after examining another man who lay prone in the dust, and Calhoun knew that would be the doctor. He was a youngish man, with a quiet air of competence about him, and was shaking his head now.

It took a second look for Calhoun, as he rode closer, to observe that the dead man, dead from a bullet, and not long before, was dressed almost exactly as he was. He too was a tall slender man with coal-black hair, and with wide open eyes of a soft, hurt, somehow bewildered brown, as though this thing that had struck him was completely beyond his comprehension or ability to deal with.

17

He too wore a blue shirt and heavy cowhide chaps, and a gun in a holster, a gun which had apparently not been drawn at all. Even his Stetson was gray like Calhoun's. And someone among the bystanders was looking down at him and voicing a puzzled question:

"But why? Why'd Doyle want to kill him? A stranger? He just got off the stage, not half an hour ago."

2

At the moment, Calhoun was too occupied with what had to be done to attach significance to the remark. The girl had spunk. He gave her credit for that. She hadn't whimpered once during the ride, though her eyes showed the increasing pain of the poison as it made itself felt, and the shock and terror of the thing was still with her.

He swung down from his horse, leaving it to stand and blow, and lifted her down, holding her in his arms like a child.

"Lead the way, Doc," he ordered brusquely. "She's been bitten by a rattler."

Doc Fenton gave them both a startled, surprised glance, and the crowd was doing the same, turning from the dead man to something of fresher interest. Disregarding them, Calhoun followed the doctor across the street and through a door, into an office, and eased the girl into a chair. The medico, he noted approvingly, was swift and dextrous. He wasted no time in setting to work.

"Where'd it happen?" he asked. "How long ago?"

"Half an hour, back a couple of miles," Calhoun explained. "Horse threw her—right between a couple of them—just about as I happened to come along."

"You applied the tourniquet, then. Anything else?"

"I sucked out the wound."

"That was using your head," the doctor said. Then, absorbed in his work, he fell silent. Calhoun watched until, satisfied that the girl was in good hands, and knowing that her chances for recovery should also be good, he went out, unnoticed. Three or four of the bystanders were just carrying the dead man off the street.

Those who still loitered eyed him with a curious intentness. Calhoun paid them little attention, since no one spoke directly to him. They knew who the girl was, of course, which would account for their interest in him.

His eyes swept the town, registering cold disapproval. Sage. The name fitted. It was a grayly bleak town in an equally gray setting. There was one big clump of cottonwoods, with a few others at the edge, a few stunted juniper on the hillsides, and a lot of sage stretching to the horizon. The alkali appeared to have ended some little distance back. Even the buildings were as raw and unlovely as their surroundings.

There was a watering trough a little farther down the street, green with moss. An old pump, its wooden spout tied in place with twisted rusty wire, stood above it. Calhoun led his horse to it and pumped water, and watched it drink, nose thrust deep into the coolness, before he slaked his own thirst. The sun was dipping toward the west, and he considered briefly whether to spend the night here, or ride on out to Lone Pine. The latter, he knew, should be another dozen or fifteen miles beyond, north and west.

Ample time remained, and by taking it easy his cayuse could make it. He wanted to get there, and that decided him. He swung to saddle again, and left town at a walk. A couple of miles out, suddenly and surprisingly, there was a tiny green valley with

a small stream running down it. It was like paradise after the last three days, and he loosened the
cinch and allowed his horse to graze for half an
hour, while he lay on his back in the grass, under
the shade which reached out from the side of the
hill, and his thoughts went back to the girl and
what had happened.

Who was she, and what had she been doing out
there, all alone? People had looked at them in a
funny sort of a way, which had left him puzzled
and more than a little irritated. Evidently she had
been back up that coulee to where the old aban-
doned house stood. It struck him as being a queer
place to ride, on such a day.

She was, quite plainly, a competent sort of person, and accustomed to looking after herself. And
well able to do so, he guessed, under most circum-
stances. What had happened to her had been an
unusual accident, a freak of chance. But if he
hadn't come along, it would have gone hard with
her.

His mind stopped then at the dead man, and
engaged in a puzzled speculation. He had been
close enough to Calhoun in build and dress for it
to be noticeable, although there were plenty of
other men who could fill that bill also.

The significant thing was that he had gotten off

the stage on which Calhoun had been riding, up to that morning—and on which, but for his sudden decision, he would still have arrived. This other man, a stranger in Sage like himself, had boarded it somewhere during the day, and had been killed in a swift-picked quarrel, from all the signs, as soon as he alighted.

Probably it didn't concern him, Calhoun decided, for there could have been reasons and recognition behind it all, whatever the bystanders thought. But he could not help having a fellow-feeling for the slain man. If he'd been on the stage instead, he might have been mistaken for this other man. Or—his eyes narrowed at the thought—had the stranger been mistaken for him? But he dismissed that as too improbable. Nobody would be interested in him in this country, even if they knew he was coming, which was unlikely.

The rest had done his cayuse a lot of good. Calhoun tightened the cinch again and rode on, and noted with approval that the country was changing now, and for the better. Here were real foot-hills at last, and though there was little timber, it was a good cattle country. And by the same token, a good country to live in, with green to rest the eyes, and the hills rolling up to break the endless gray monotony of sun-scorched prairie. Even the air here had a different, more vitalizing quality to it.

Which made it all the more surprising that a girl, if she wanted to go for a ride, would pick the section lying east out of Sage, instead of turning back in among these hills.

A tall, barren hill reared off at the left, half a mile beyond the wagon road. A little used trail skirted the foot of it, and after studying it briefly, Calhoun swung onto it. It was a short cut, used occasionally, he judged, by men on horseback anxious to save a mile or so. The hill itself was of shale, which appeared to have covered the trail several times, pushing it farther out. So the road took the longer, safer route.

"Wouldn't take much to start a bad slide there," Calhoun nodded to himself. "I can see why most folks steer clear of the cut-off."

Half a score miles out from town, he reached a creek—the first sizeable stream that he had seen for days. It was wide and swift, brawling down from the north, and most of it seemed to run between high, rocky ledges. There was more timber to the west.

Here the canyon flattened out to a crossing, a ford so swift and deep that his horse had almost to swim. Calhoun lifted his feet from the stirrups, and the force of the current carried his cayuse, snorting, a full fifty feet downstream while he crossed.

A couple of miles beyond, he sighted Lone Pine.

Calhoun knew it at once from the great single pine tree that stood, sentinel-like, on the flat bluff just back of the clustered buildings. It was a massive tree, twisted by storms, dwarfing the lesser evergreens on the slope below. The big log house had a comfortable, weathered look, with a big porch running around it on two sides. There was a bunk house off a little distance, a bigger barn and corrals behind.

He studied them carefully, aware that a sort of destiny had led him here, and found the place, on the whole, rather better than he had expected. There were a few horses in the corrals, and he could see the brand on their left hips—a representation of the Lone Pine.

But it was the people in sight whom he studied intently. Buildings, cattle and horses, land, were always somewhat similar, never too hard to understand or to deal with. But men and women were a different proposition, each one presenting a new and vital problem, and there were four of them in sight as he approached.

One man sat in a rocking chair on the big porch and rocked with a thumping noise where the floor was uneven, keeping it up with a steady persistency that could soon become annoying. He was a man with thinning silvery hair and a sharp, fox-like face, and a blanket lay draped across his lap. He clutched a crutch in both hands and used it to help him rock, and close at hand stood a wheel-chair, empty. Evidently he had transferred from one to the other, and Calhoun guessed that his legs were crippled.

The other three men lounged by the bunk house, on a stretch of grass, evidently just in from the day's work and relaxing a little before supper. One was combing his hair without the aid of a mirror. He was a chunky, square-built man as he sat there, legs stretched before him, and his hair was thick and wiry and butter-colored. His eyes, as he raised them at Calhoun's approach, were sullen and some-how resentful, filled with a suspicion which seemed to include the whole world. He wore a six-gun in an open holster.

Beside him, flat on his back, hat pulled over his face, was a wiry little oldster, who sat up suddenly, bantam-like, at the sound of hoofs, and regarded Calhoun in warm, friendly appraisal, his blue eyes crinkling. The third man was a youngster, seven-teen at the most, but big, clumsy and uncertain, and he eyed Calhoun with a doubtful hostility.

These were probably his crew, Calhoun reflected, and a poor lot they looked to be. The oldster would be a good man so far as he was able, but his days for hard work were long past. The other two were doubtful additions at best, and irritation surged in him again. Why ask a man to take a job with such help?

Then he saw another man coming out of the bunk house, and knew instantly that he was of different caliber. He walked with an easy assurance, and he was tall and lean and quiet. Besides that, he packed two guns openly, and his clothes, like his boots, were expensive.

He came up as Calhoun dismounted, his glance inquiring, and it seemed to Calhoun that, for just a flickering instant, there was surprise in his eyes as well, but it was quickly hidden.

"This is the Lone Pine, isn't it?" Calhoun asked.

"That's right," was the brief reply.

"I'm lookin' for the owner," Calhoun added.

"I'm the owner. And you're Mr. Calhoun?"

Calhoun turned, startled. It was a woman who had spoken, and she had just come around the corner of the house, on the porch. She was standing near the wheel-chair, eying him levelly from straight gray eyes, under loosely piled, golden brown hair. She was tall for a woman, though not too tall—and twenty-two or thereabouts. She wore a short dress, built for riding, and spurred boots. And all this, her good looks, her obvious competence, and most of all, her declaration that she was the owner, took him aback and filled him with a swift irritation.

"I'm Calhoun," he admitted, and his animosity was in his voice. "I didn't know that a woman owned Lone Pine."

A touch of angry color came into the girl's cheeks, but she kept her voice cool.

"This is my uncle," she said. "Sam Troupe." She nodded very slightly toward the man in the chair. "Mr. Calhoun, Uncle. And these are our crew." She indicated them briefly. "John Wyss— who has been acting as foreman until you got here." That was the newcomer, the man who wore two guns.

"Schuyler Muskett," she went on, and the youngster bobbed his head uncertainly, coming to his feet and stumbling over them in the process.

"Bill Bailey—" The old-timer grinned and came nimbly to his feet. "And Harry Glades." The sullen man neither stood up nor spoke, but nodded briefly.

She had spoken swiftly, almost as if to forestall any chance at interruption. She added a word of plainly unnecessary explanation now.

"Mr. Calhoun has come here to be foreman, boys."

Anger had been mounting in Calhoun. If there was one thing that he disliked, it was to be tricked. He'd had a good job, as top hand, back where he had been. The letter had come, signed M. J. Johnson, offering him the job of foreman of the Lone Pine Ranch. And so he had come here to take the job. But how was a man to guess from the initials that M. J. Johnson would be a woman?

"There's been a mistake," he said tightly. "I'm not working for a woman."

He saw the red flame swiftly in the girl's cheeks, and was glad of her anger. To him this meant more than a week's time wasted, the disappointment of not becoming a foreman after all, and the humiliation to which, wittingly or otherwise, she had subjected him. But before she could answer, the man in the chair exploded in a cackle of shrill laughter.

"Hear that, Marjorie?" he chuckled. "Won't work for a woman! Tee-hee!" He turned to Calhoun for the first time, and there was something like venom in his tones.

"Won't work for a woman, eh? That's the spirit I like in a man. Ain't many got it, these days. But I reckon she's got you cinched this time, young feller. How about that contract you signed, eh? Agreein' to act as foreman of Lone Pine for a year? Forgettin' that, ain't ye?"

Calhoun knew, instantly and definitely, that he did not like Sam Troupe. He sensed in the same moment, despite his rising anger, that Marjorie Johnson did not like her uncle, either. Her face had gone still redder, then a strained white.

Without a word, she reached inside her dress and drew out a paper which Calhoun recognized as the contract he had signed—and which, for one hot moment, he had forgotten. Resentment grew in him. It was just like a woman to get a man to sign a contract by that sort of misrepresentation, then to hold him to it against his will.

"This is your contract, Mr. Calhoun—to work here as foreman for one year." The cool scorn in her tones stung him. Deliberately, she tore it across and across, then sent the remnants fluttering. "That's gone. I certainly wouldn't think of holding you on it, if you wouldn't serve without it. What I want to hire is loyalty—that or nothing!"

3

Calhoun was startled, taken aback. His resentment evaporated, to be replaced by an unwilling admiration. This girl, despite his first impression that she had deliberately worked to trick him into signing that contract, played it square, straight from the shoulder, like a man. Her uncle was staring nonplussed at the last bit of paper fluttering to the ground. The scorn, and an open challenge, was still in the girl's eyes as she dusted her hands.

"If that's the way you feel about it," Calhoun said slowly, "and want me to stay, why—I've changed my mind. And when I take a job, I work at it."

Marjorie smiled suddenly, and held out her hand. It was tanned and calloused, he noted, and she had a grip like a man.

"That's a deal, Mr. Calhoun," she agreed. "I'm sorry if there was any misunderstanding to start with. I didn't intend it that way. I've signed all my letters M. J. Johnson for quite a while."

"Sure changed his mind in a hurry, after he saw what a pretty gal he'd be workin' for, didn't he?" Sam Troupe cackled again. Marjorie flushed a little, more with annoyance than anything else, Calhoun guessed, but her voice was as level as ever when she spoke.

"I'm afraid you'll be getting chilly, Uncle. Schuyler, help him inside, please."

The boy came up on the porch, stumbling awkwardly, and Troupe flashed him a look of open dislike. But Calhoun could see the hero-worship in this boy for his employer, a sort of dumb worship, and he stooped and lifted Troupe from the rocking chair to the wheel-chair with an easy off-handedness, paying no attention to the angry sputtering of the man. Then he wheeled him around the corner of the porch and out of sight.

"Bill, show Mr. Calhoun where things are," Marjorie instructed, and turned back inside the house. The oldster, spry and grinning, fell into step beside Calhoun, leading the way to the barn and then in turn to the bunk house.

"Don't blame you for feelin' as you done, Calhoun," he said. "Most folks feels that way, I guess, 'bout workin' for a woman. But Marjorie, she ain't no ordinary person in skirts. No siree-bob! You've got you a job, but looks to me like she picked her a man for the job, at that. There's grub call. You better wash up and come eat."

Calhoun did so, removing some of the grime of the long ride. He followed Bailey into the big log house, where it was apparent that everyone ate together. There he was introduced to Mrs. Henry, the housekeeper, a motherly sort of a woman who eyed him through a pair of steel-rimmed spectacles and then held out a plump hand for him to shake.

"I like a man that speaks his mind—and can have the grace to change it, too," she said directly.

Calhoun could feel a constraint at the table. He tried to remove it, talking with Marjorie and Mrs. Henry, and Bailey joined in. So too, did Wyss, but Glades ate in heavy, unbroken silence, and Muskett was plainly bashful and ill at ease. Behind it all, Calhoun sensed, was some sort of trouble, though what it might be, he had no idea.

All he knew was that he'd been working for Paul Bowman of Muleshoe, a top hand on a mighty fine ranch. Bowman had received a letter from M. J. Johnson of Lone Pine, saying that he—though it had been the impersonal I—had often heard Bowman referred to as a competent cattleman and an honest one. Which, Calhoun knew, was no exaggeration.

The letter had gone on to say that Lone Pine stood in need of a foreman—a thoroughly competent man who could handle a big job. And it had ended by requesting Bowman to recommend some good man for the job.

Bowman had shown him the letter, and his answer recommending him.

"I'll hate to lose you, Calhoun," he had said. "But it looks like a good job, and it's a big step up."

The answer had come back, along with a year's contract. That was all he knew about the job.

The meal ended, the others filed out. Marjorie's uncle had not appeared for supper, and Calhoun guessed that he was probably sulking in his room. At a glance from Marjorie, he lingered, then followed her into the next room, which was an office, with a big desk and mounted game heads ranged on the walls. A bearskin rug was on the floor, a grizzly. She caught his glance and explained.

"My father shot them all," she said. And, seated in the big swivel chair, looking almost lost in it, she studied him for a long moment with silent intentness. Calhoun met the gaze, and suddenly she smiled, though the smile was gone again as quickly.

"I don't think I've made any mistake," she said quietly. "Mr. Bowman said that you were a man who could handle whatever situation came along, however tough it might be, and that you'd fight your way through to the end."

"When I take a job, I try to do it," Calhoun repeated.

"I'm sure of it. . . . Maybe I owe you another apology. Maybe it isn't quite fair to you, to get you in here, to take a job that you know nothing about, which is difficult—and probably dangerous. But I give you my word that I didn't know it would be so bad when I wrote to you. Things were shaping up, but they've gotten much worse the last few days. If you don't want to stay—"

"Let's forget that angle of it," Calhoun said. "I'm foreman here now."

"Thanks. You see, I had to have someone who was new to this country. I knew that. Someone I could trust. From all that I'd heard about Paul Bowman, I knew that any man he recommended would be all right. And I didn't know anyone, personally, that I could turn to."

"Just what's the trouble, anyway?" Calhoun asked.

"They're trying to run me off Lone Pine," Marjorie answered. "When I wrote to you, it was just talk, rather vague, but I knew that it was shaping up for trouble. Since then, it has come to a head. The three biggest outfits in this section of country are back of it. There's Vick—Abelard Vick, of the Wagon Wheel. He's back of it all. And Abel, of the Flying A Ranch. Harkness, of the Window Sash, is the other one."

"Run you off?" Calhoun repeated. "But how can they do that?" He looked around, out the window, and some of his surprise was in his voice. "This looks like an old, settled place."

"It's all due to a mix-up in titles," Marjorie explained. "It is an old settled place. My father came in here and settled over nineteen years ago. He got a title from the authorities soon after, and was satisfied that it was good, up to the day of his death, a few months ago. There were several such titles issued around the country, and no one questioned them until recently.

"But lately it has been brought up, and there has been trouble. Vick is back of it all, I know. He's been trying to get hold of Lone Pine from the start, by any means he could think of." Her face colored. "He thought he could manage it by marrying me, but I didn't see it that way. So now he's trying other methods. Lone Pine is the best ranch in this whole section of country."

From what little he had seen of it, and the country back in here, Calhoun could easily believe that.

"The three of them brought up the question of titles, and I still thought that the title of Lone Pine was good. But the whole question was taken to court, and it seems there are flaws. Records weren't kept very well, back nearly twenty years ago. Some have been lost entirely. A lot of titles were open to question. So the state and county and federal authorities worked out a scheme between them, that seemed fair enough. For those places—including Lone Pine—where it seemed that the title had been good, and had been accepted as such for so many years, but where it was impossible to prove it, they set up a general rule. For any place that had been held for twenty years, the title would be validated and made legal."

"Twenty years," Calhoun repeated. "And you say your father settled here somethin' over nineteen years ago?"

"About nineteen years and six months," Marjorie

agreed. "And the agreement is that land which has *not* been held for twenty years is supposed to be free land—open land. At least that's what Vick and Abel and Harkness claim. They all want a slice of Lone Pine. I think they deliberately managed to get that twenty-year proviso inserted, and all the rest of it, just so they could grab it."

"And now they're tryin' to?"

"Now they're trying to," she nodded. "They've had a meeting, just the last few days, and declared that Lone Pine and three smaller outfits, all on this side of Cayuse Creek—you crossed it a couple of miles back—are not held by any legal title, and so are open for the taking—by anyone strong enough to take and hold them, though they don't say it just that way. They've declared Cayuse Creek is the deadline—and any and all outfits of questionable title west of the deadline, open for the taking. They're doing it that way so that it won't look quite so obvious that it's all aimed at Lone Pine."

"Have they tried to run you off yet?"

"Not yet. They offered to buy me out—for a tenth of what it's worth. I told them that I'd fight —and hold Lone Pine! If I'm still in possession when the twenty-year limit they set is up, or six months from now, I'll get clear title despite all they can do. So they aim to run me off before then, of course. They set a time limit, too—which starts tomorrow!"

She was breathing quickly, her face flushed, as she leaned toward him.

"I'm glad you're here! There's not a man in this country that I could trust for such a job—not a man who is competent, who would take the job against those three outfits!"

Calhoun frowned out the window. This was different from anything he had expected, and challenging. He admired Marjorie Johnson for her determination to fight and hold on to what was hers. Since she was a girl, with an obviously inadequate crew, the others had probably figured that it would be easy to rob her, that a show of force would be all that would be required.

"If you take the job, the way things are now," she went on quietly, "it will be dangerous. I don't think they'd kill me—merely try to get me off. But with you, they'll have no compunctions."

"Probably not," Calhoun agreed. "You say this Vick wanted to marry you?"

"Yes. He still insists that he's going to. He had the gall to tell me, just the other day, that they were going to take Lone Pine—and that I'd have to marry him then to get it back!"

"Sounds right conceited," Calhoun nodded. "I've heard of a lot of schemes for stealin', but this is a little different. Gives them a sort of legal cloak, the way they're working it. And I suppose the rest of the country is scared to buck them?"

"Scared is the word," Marjorie said contemptuously. "Three or four little fellows have been scared out already, though their title was as good as mine. They've sold out for a song and left the country."

"And these other three, this side of deadline? What about them?"

"They're frightened, too," she confessed. "So far, they haven't been bluffed clear out. They're waiting for you to arrive, I think, to see what you intend to do before they decide."

"And what plans did *you* have?" Calhoun challenged.

Marjorie shook her head.

"None—except to fight, and hold what's my own."

"And that crew's all you've got?"

"That's all," she agreed. "As I say, if you don't want to take the risk—"

"I'm taking it," he said sharply. "I said I'd take the job, and when I give my word, I keep it." His tone softened a little. "If you can fight, I guess I can do the same. You said Wyss was foreman.

Why didn't you keep him at that job? He looks
like he knew his business."

"He does," Marjorie agreed. "But I'm sure that
he isn't the man for the job—now."

"But you're keepin' him on as a hand?"

"I have been. You can hire and fire as you please
—with the exception of Bill Bailey. He's a good,
loyal man, and has been with Lone Pine since my
father first came here. I couldn't let Bill go."

That gave him his answer. She had no more confidence in the crew than he had, and had kept them
simply because she had no notion where to get
any who would be better. It was not a cheering
prospect.

But he had given his word, and the challenge of
the situation intrigued him. He talked for another
hour, getting some background knowledge of the
ranch and its affairs, being shown the books. He saw
that Marjorie was resolved to trust him implicitly,
to leave the handling of the ranch and this situation in his hands. She had been assured for years
that Paul Bowman was an honest man whose judgment could be trusted, and Bowman had recommended him. But his former boss had had no notion
of how tough a job he'd be up against. Calhoun
smiled to himself, a little wryly, as he said good
night.

41

The moon was not yet up, and the night was dark. He crossed to the bunk house and let himself in quietly, moving to the bunk where he had already unrolled his blankets. Snores greeted him. He pulled his boots off; then, ears attuned to the interior of the room and eyes to the gloom, he looked around more sharply.

Bailey and Glades were both asleep. But neither Wyss nor Muskett were in their bunks, nor anywhere around. And neither man had any good reason or excuse for being absent now, without having said a word to him.

Calhoun hesitated. Then he pulled on his boots again and slipped silently back into the night.

4

There was not much to do but wait and see, and Calhoun waited with a resigned patience, leaning back against the trunk of a big cottonwood, his mind busy with what he had learned so far. Viewed dispassionately, it impressed him as a job so big as to be next to hopeless. These others had decided, coolly enough, to move in on Lone Pine and take it over. And what was there to stop them, aside from a woman's resolution not to give up to them, and his own determination to help her?

Ordinarily there would be law to appeal to, but

here the big three stood in no danger of apprehension by the law. Public opinion was quiescent, or frightened. He had a crew on his hands which impressed him as being of little use, and probably, from the present look of things, with one or more traitors in it.

The moon came up, a thin sliver of silver, stealing like a frightened night bird above the rim of the valley, climbing among the wavering stars. A whippoorwill moved on ghost wings among the host of insects which appeared to dance before the moon, and somewhere a cow bawled restlessly. A horse stamped in the barn, and hoofs sounded with a muted cadence, coming not from the road, but across a sodden field.

The rider dismounted, stripped off the saddle and turned his horse into the corrals. He bulked, vague against the light, as he moved toward the bunk house, and the door of it opened and closed softly. That was Wyss. And his horse, standing, head hanging, in a corner of the corral, showed the dark marks of sweat.

Another ten minutes, and a second horseman appeared, coming this time by road. Muskett moved with a clumsy haste, and his hand fumbled at the bunk house door. But his cayuse showed no signs of having been ridden hard or far, and Calhoun pondered this a while, in growing puzzlement. He stood at one of the open windows of the bunk house, very patient, until his ears told him that both newcomers were asleep. Then he let himself in and pulled off his boots for the second time.

He spent another hour in the morning going over the affairs of the ranch with Marjorie, and found them no more to his liking than any of the rest of the situation. Lone Pine was a big ranch, and a good one, so far as he could judge. By rights, it should have been prosperous.

But the facts proved otherwise. Declining rather than expanding herds, a bit of trouble here, another bit there. Little things which, added all together, amounted to a big one.

"I've done the best I knew, the last months," Marjorie confessed to him, a little hopelessly. "But things just haven't seemed to work out right. I don't know just where the trouble is."

Calhoun had a hunch about what was wrong. There was a traitor here, who was so placed that he could constantly make things go wrong. There could be no other explanation. Vick, of course, had wanted Lone Pine for a long while, and had been working to undermine it, to cause it to collapse. When other methods had proved too slow, he had thought of this deadline idea, and had found neighbors enough who were voracious where there was a prospect of spoils.

He returned to the bunk house, where Glades and Muskett both loafed, awaiting his orders. Bailey was at work in the tool shed, whistling cheerfully, mending a bridle, and Wyss had occupied himself in the barn, currying horses and cleaning out. He nodded to the two of them, and they followed him to the bunk house.

"I think you all know what we're up against here," Calhoun said without preamble. "Deadline has been set, both as to time and place. And we're on the wrong side, both ways. That's going to mean trouble, and plenty of it, or I miss my guess."

He paused a moment, watching their faces for a reaction, but there was none. Glades was still sullen, watching him out of narrowed eyes. Bailey whistled tunelessly, almost soundlessly, under his breath. Muskett looked from Calhoun to Wyss and back again, and Wyss watched Calhoun with a quick, appraising show of interest.

"Since that's what we're up against, we all need to know where we stand, right now," Calhoun went on. "I know that some of you resent me being brought in here as foreman. I can understand that. I didn't know about the job, didn't go after it.

But I took it, and I aim to stay on as foreman of Lone Pine for at least the year that I first signed up for—and that means past deadline."

He paused again, but no one spoke. He went on, his voice a little sharper.

"You've been working here, drawing Miss Johnson's pay. When a man takes pay, he's supposed to give loyalty in return. So I'm assuming that you've been doing just that. But it's going to be a tough job from here on out, and some of us are apt to get hurt before it's over with. If any of you don't want to stay, conditions being what they are, you can pull out now—and I'll figure that it's because you don't care to work with me, and no hard feelings. But whoever does stay, I'll expect you to work with me, and for Lone Pine—and no quitting in a pinch."

"That's fair enough," Bailey spoke up. "And I'm trailin' along with you."

"There's not many of us to start with," Wyss said pleasantly. "We can't afford to make things harder by quitting now. As you say, we've been taking wages here, and we owe something in return."

"I'll stick," Muskett said, eying Wyss a little uncertainly. There was either hero-worship here, and the tendency still to look to his former foreman for orders, or something else. Calhoun was not sure which.

"Count me in," Glades growled. "I don't like the set-up, but I don't quit in a pinch."

There was blunt honesty in that, and the man went up a notch in Calhoun's estimation. He spoke briskly.

"That's fine. There's plenty here that I don't know, and I'm depending on you boys to help me out. Just how much time we have to get set in, before the others start something, I don't know. As I understand it, today is deadline. But they probably will wait a little while to see what we're going to do before they start pushing. After all, there's no great rush on their part."

Muskett spoke up unexpectedly.

"I hear tell that the three of 'em—Vick, an' Harkness, an' Abel—are meetin' in town late this afternoon, most likely to talk it over."

"That's interesting," Calhoun murmured, and wondered where Muskett had gained the information. Wyss shot a quick look at him, either of surprise or possibly displeasure; and, meeting it, Muskett flushed redly.

"You boys know what work there is to be done today better than I do," Calhoun went on. "So I'm going to ask you to go ahead and do it, as you know it needs to be done. And keep a sharp lookout for trouble—of any sort, from any quarter! It might be just as well to ride two and two from now on, and for one man to stick around the buildings here all the time. So if you'll stay around here today, Bill, that'll be fine. I want to look things over, and I'll need a guide. How about doing that, Muskett?"

"You're the boss," the boy mumbled.

Calhoun had chosen him deliberately. He would rather have had Bill Bailey for guide, but Bailey would be a dependable man to leave here, and he wanted to talk to Muskett. As they came out, he had a glimpse of Sam Troupe propelling himself out on to the porch in his wheel-chair, directing a tirade over his shoulder to some invisible person, probably Marjorie.

They rode, swinging north, the boy silent and a little sullen, but the clumsiness and lack of grace had fallen away from him as he swung into saddle. He was perfectly at home on horseback, a good hand, Calhoun guessed.

Moreover, he knew the country, and, thawing a little as Calhoun talked in friendly fashion and made no effort to question him, he began to point out things and to explain as they went along. Calhoun saw that he took a deep pride, deep down, in Lone Pine.

Cayuse Creek provided the biggest surprise. Mile on mile it ran, encased in a rocky gorge, brawling along in a succession of rapids and waterfalls. And at the rare points where it did run peacefully between low banks, there was a sort of deceptive smoothness. Muskett nodded casually at one of these.

"That Cayuse sure ain't never been broken," he said. "Looks peaceful, right over there—but you can't cross. Quicksand. It's that way all along. Mighty few spots where a man or horse can get across at all."

Calhoun considered that. Marjorie had not mentioned it, probably because she was so familiar with the situation that she had not even thought about it. But Cayuse might prove a deadline in more ways than one, if only he had a bigger crew. A barrier to keep the others out. If they could cross at only two or three places along the stretching miles—

"There's Ogg's place," Muskett said suddenly, pointing. "He's one of the small ones that's on the wrong side of deadline, along with us. Think his name used to be Hogg, but he didn't like it and dropped the H when he come here. Didn't change him much." He shrugged, with a boy's uncompromising certainty. "Looks like he's quittin' and gettin' out, while the going's good."

Calhoun studied the place. It was a small outfit at best, and Ogg had been running it all alone. It looked it. A small barn, a smaller shack, corrals, all rather unkempt, showed where one man had tried to do too much and had failed to get a great deal of anything accomplished.

There was a broken down wagon, left standing among weeds where a wheel had collapsed. Two logs were off one side of the corral. The rusty stovepipe, protruding through the roof of the shack, leaned at a crazy angle.

A wagon stood beside the house, and Ogg, heavy, slow-moving, somehow indecisive, was carrying out his belongings and loading them onto the wagon, piling it high in haphazard fashion, a harassed look on his whisker-stubbled face.

As they rode closer, he looked up in nervous apprehension and lumbered toward a rifle which leaned against the side of the house. Then, recognizing Muskett, he hesitated and waited, still too far away from the gun to do any good if there had been treachery intended.

Beneath the heavy folds of flesh was a furtive, weak look and watery eyes. He nodded heavily to Muskett in response to the latter's hail, but kept his gaze fixed on Calhoun.

"This is Calhoun, Lone Pine's new foreman, Bert," Muskett explained. "What's going on? You ain't being bluffed out, are you?"

"I ain't aimin' to be a fool and stay," Ogg said heavily. "What chance has a man got, stayin' past deadline?"

"Mr. Calhoun's aimin' to fight," Muskett said. "We ain't givin' Lone Pine up."

Ogg shrugged.

"That way, you'll just get killed," he said. "They're too strong for us. But you can do as you like. I'm gettin' out."

"If we all worked together, we'd be strong enough to hold them off and win," Calhoun spoke up. "It looks to me like you've been in here quite a while, and worked hard."

"Seven years," Ogg agreed bitterly. "And all for nothin'. I slave to get things fixed nice an' comfortable, an' what do I get out of it?"

Muskett snickered, and strangled on it, but Calhoun kept a straight face, and Ogg did not notice.

"It doesn't need to be that way," Calhoun said. "I'm going on and see Sackett and DeMers. Why should four outfits let three run them out?"

Ogg pondered this, undecided. The arithmetic was good, even if the logic was poor, but Calhoun had used the argument deliberately, foreseeing that it would impress Ogg, that he would not reason it through. He nodded slowly.

"I never thought of it in just that way before," he confessed. "That's right, though. There are four of us to three of them."

"Sure," Calhoun agreed cheerfully. "If it was me, I'd hate to be chased off land I'd worked for for seven years. And I suppose you're a lot closer than that to a title."

"Yeah, I am," Ogg conceded, fingering his stubbled chin. "I got this place from old man Rowe. He'd had it twelve years. Twelve an' seven are nineteen, I guess. All counts for me, too."

"And lacks only a year of giving you a clear title," Calhoun prompted.

"Yeah. So it does. But they warned me to get out—or get planted." He hesitated, thinking heavily. "You say you're goin' to talk to the others?"

"I aim to. We'll do better to work together."

"That makes sense." Ogg looked around, and came to a decision, which was obviously difficult for him. "Reckon in that case, I'll stay—at least till I hear what they got to say." Anger flared in him, the slow anger of a stubborn man. "They ain't got no right to tell me what to do or where I got to go."

He was unloading the stuff from the wagon again as Calhoun rode on. Calhoun sent Muskett back to the ranch house with instructions to move a bunch of the cattle, whom they had found here where the feed was poor, and headed on up the valley toward where DeMers' outfit lay.

It was bigger than Ogg's, Muskett explained, for DeMers kept two cowhands, and a man like that would be more apt to fight than quit. Likewise, he was progressive, orderly, and getting ahead.

This was wilder, more broken mountain country; the air was thin and high, the sunlight diffused. A far cry from the bleak prairie he had crossed the day before. But Cayuse, off at the side, was a wilder creek than ever. He understood now why it had been named deadline. It was an appropriate barrier, either way.

And in the past, it had shut the other outfits out from this choicer land west of the water line. No wonder they coveted it, lying on the prairie's rim. But Cayuse could again be a double deadline.

He had ridden on for a mile, and was out of sight of Ogg's sorry outfit, when he heard the sound, sharp and clear. A rifle, from back where he had come.

Startled, Calhoun swung his horse. There was no other sound, but he had a hunch that it would be well to investigate. Not that it seemed likely to Calhoun that there would be any real threat to Ogg, at least not yet. He was small in the scheme of things, hesitant and easily bluffed. And if it came to a crisis, that would be far better for their purpose than any more drastic measures.

But his unease mounted as he came in sight of the decrepit buildings again. Nothing moved there now; the wagon still stood, half unloaded. Then, half a mile away to the west, he saw a horseman just vanishing among a clump of trees.

He saw Ogg next, sprawled face down in the dust, still clutching a battered chair which he had been carrying back to the house. He had been shot in the back, and apparently he had never known what hit him, nor guessed at the imminence of danger.

5

Cold fury shook Calhoun. This was murder, wanton and deliberate, as uncalled for as it was unjustified. It showed one thing. The warning to Ogg to get out or get planted had been given in deadly earnest, and his death had been intended as a further warning to Lone Pine and the others on the wrong side of deadline to quit or die.

That other rider had seen, of course, that Ogg had decided to heed the warning, had started to pack up and move. And that he had changed his mind, and was unloading his stuff again. That decision, to tarry a while, had cost him his life.

In a way, Calhoun felt responsible for what had

happened. Ogg would not have reconsidered save for what he had told him. Yet no sane man could have anticipated such an unprovoked and completely useless murder.

Apparently the killer was a lone hand, as he had seen in the distance, someone who had crossed the Cayuse and was spying on them. Had he been with anyone, he would not have so callously shot an unsuspecting man in the back. It was likewise pretty clear that he had come too late to see Calhoun or Muskett, and so had believed himself all alone thereabouts.

One look confirmed that Ogg was dead. There was nothing that Calhoun could do for him, and he lost no time in spurring after the killer. There was risk in what he did, and he took it deliberately. If the killer suspected that he had been a virtual witness to what had happened, he would try to ambush him in turn.

But that was unlikely, and to wait was to insure the man's escape. Calhoun reached the spot where he had glimpsed the horseman. There he found a dim trail through the patch of scraggly evergreens, but it had swung abruptly east again, and when at length he reached the river, he saw that the killer had re-crossed it, swimming his horse at a spot which looked completely impassable.

There was no point in following. The fugitive was too far ahead to be overtaken or identified now. Calhoun returned to the ranch buildings, and ate. He told Bill Bailey what had happened, and dispatched him and Muskett to bury Ogg. It was the least he could do.

Troupe was not on the shady side of the porch. He learned, from a remark of Mrs. Henry, that the crippled man had locked himself in his room and was apparently sulking there. That, he guessed, was a trick in which he frequently indulged.

Well, being tied to a chair would curdle the disposition of most men, Calhoun reflected, and did not blame him too much. He saddled a fresh horse and set out for Sage, mindful of what Muskett had told him. If the Big Three, as they were called, were going to discuss the campaign against Lone Pine, he might as well attend the meeting himself. The fact that he hadn't been invited did not trouble him.

He reached Sage at mid-afternoon; a few lazy clouds swooped overhead and seemed to accentuate the heat by their brief interludes of shade. Inquiry revealed that Harkness was the only one of the three yet in town. Calhoun's informant added a bit of rather startling news.

"He's over to Mis' Abernathy's now, with his

daughter. You was the one that brought her in yesterday, wasn't you? She's gettin' along well as can be expected, the doc says. Reckon the old man 'll be plumb grateful to you for helpin' her, too. Sets a right smart store by his girl."

Calhoun digested this. So the girl whom he had helped was the daughter of Harkness, of the Window Sash—and Harkness was one of the Three! That put a new light on things. If Harkness was grateful—and he had reason to be—that might be turned to the advantage of Lone Pine. It would do no harm to drop in at Mrs. Abernathy's and meet Harkness.

He turned down-street, and stopped. A cayuse was tied at the hitch-rail in front of a saloon, in the shade of a big cottonwood. Despite the shade, it stood with drooping head, and it was lathered with sweat. And there was something curiously familiar about it.

Calhoun had had only a glimpse of the killer's horse, disappearing in the distance, but now his suspicions were mounting. This horse, he saw, wore the brand of Wagon Wheel, which belonged to Abelard Vick—and Vick was the kingpin of the Three, the man who had been so long intent on getting hold of Lone Pine by whatever means presented itself.

Calhoun entered the saloon. He paused a moment in the doorway, to accustom his eyes to the semi-darkness after the bright sun outside. He was aware that a sudden hush had fallen at his entrance, that every eye was fixed on him. There were about a dozen men in the room, and they were looking from him to another man who was standing at the bar and toying with a half filled glass, and who also was watching him now with sharpened attention.

This man, Calhoun was sure, was the rider of the horse. He was a man fully three inches taller than Calhoun, and with a heavy, beefy frame to match. Muscular rather than fat, and tough-looking. He had light yellow hair, close cropped, a darker yellow mustache and thin eyebrows which gave him a slightly surprised, rather sardonic impression. But he wore no gun, at least openly, and there had been no rifle on the saddle. Which did not necessarily mean anything.

Calhoun walked to the bar, pausing a couple of steps from him, and ordered a drink. He toyed with it, set it down again. As he had expected, he did not have long to wait. This other man had an arrogance which amounted to conceit, and it came to the fore now. He sidled a step closer.

"You're the new boss of Lone Pine, I take it—Calhoun?"

Calhoun eyed him levelly.

"What of it?"

"My name's Doyle—Trouble, Trouble, Doyle and More Trouble, they call me. Of Wagon Wheel."

Calhoun waited, remembering. It was Doyle who had killed that man who had gotten off the stage the day before! Another killing without reason or provocation, according to the onlookers' reports. Calhoun said nothing, and his expressionless face seemed to irritate Doyle, who went on, a little sneeringly:

"I hear tell you've taken a job—with a woman boss. Hell of a job for a man."

"That's your opinion, is it?" Calhoun did not add that he had held much the same opinion, up to the day before.

"Ain't it the opinion of any man with guts? But don't get me wrong, Calhoun. I know about the deal they roped you in on. Contract to try and save an outfit's that sunk already. Hell of a way to treat a man. But you don't have to stand for it."

"You suggestin' somethin'?" Calhoun asked.

"I don't talk just to hear my tongue wag. That job was played out 'fore you ever took it. But there's as good a job waitin' for you with an outfit that's big and getting bigger. I mean the Wagon Wheel."

"And the Wheel aims to roll over everything in its way, eh?"

"That's the idea. Anything that gets in the way gets smashed. Better get in on the right side while the getting's good."

"I've known of wagons getting bogged down," Calhoun retorted. "And as to working for a woman—maybe I like that."

Doyle stared, his brows lifting.

"Guess you're a bigger fool than I took you for," he said shortly. "Take a piece of good advice. This ain't a healthy country for fools."

"And it's not going to be a healthy country for killers—not any longer," Calhoun said softly.

Doyle stared, and his face went a little white.

"Listen, hombre," he said. "That fellow that got off the stage yesterday tried to pull on me first—"

"So it really was you, eh?" Calhoun murmured. "And the poor bugger happened to be dressed like me—and to have gotten on that stage after I got off it. I'm beginnin' to see the way you cowardly killers work."

He knew from the sudden raging fury in Doyle's face that he had hit the mark. Doyle's hand dropped part way to his hip, then came away.

"Nobody talks to me like that when I'm packin' a gun," he growled. "But that damn marshal made me give it up when I came in today—after what happened yesterday."

It was Calhoun's turn to sneer now.

"Do you have to have a gun?" he taunted. "Or don't you use fists?"

"With you wearin' hardware? I ain't that big a fool!"

Deliberately, Calhoun unbuckled his gun belt, tossed it to the staring bartender.

"Whether you're a fool or not, you strike me as being a yellow-bellied killer," he said. "And what are you going to do about it?"

Belatedly, the bartender screeched a protest.

"Not in here, gentlemen," he implored. "Not in here. If you want to fight, take it outside—"

Calhoun was willing. He had provoked the fight deliberately, partly because a stranger had died in his place the day before, and that murder, a gunman striking without warning, had been intended to put him in his grave. And he was equally certain that this swaggering, cold-eyed bully had murdered Ogg today.

It was too good an opportunity to miss, the chance at him without his gun. Not that Calhoun was afraid of him with a gun. He might be softer that way than this, for he outweighed Calhoun and would probably be a tough antagonist. But the man had a thrashing coming, and there was cool deliberation behind Calhoun's move. If he could administer a beating to this man, who was plainly Vick's right-hand man and the prime mover in the whole thing, that would impress friends and foes alike, give him the prestige which he had to have if he was to stand a chance in the coming contest.

Doyle paid no heed to the bartender. He whipped off his coat in one quick motion and made as if to toss it aside, and instead, flung it over Calhoun's head. His intent was to confuse and blind him, and the next instant, moving with speed, he had snatched up a heavy chair and was raising it high, aiming to bring it down in a murderous blow on Calhoun's skull.

But Calhoun was not so easily caught. He had recognized the ruthlessness in the man, the treachery, as twice demonstrated already. He flung up an arm and swept the coat aside before it could envelop him, and as Doyle half turned and grabbed the chair, Calhoun whipped in at him. He kicked out viciously, his boot catching Doyle on the ankles, and off-balance, sending him crashing headlong to the floor.

Calhoun knew then that it was to be a dirty fight, with nothing barred. But if Doyle wanted it that way, it was all right with him. Doyle had gone down hard, but he was as hard as nails and quick as a striking snake. Even as he hit the floor and slid, he twisted, flung the chair, and it crashed against Calhoun's face and chest as he started to charge in.

One foot of the heavy chair struck his forehead glancingly, just above his eye, and blood spurted. He had flung up his arm again to check it, but had succeeded only in part. It dazed him momentarily, the blood ran into his eye and made it almost useless, and Doyle was on his feet again and rushing to grab his advantage, snatching at a second chair as he came.

Groggy from the blow, almost out on his feet, Calhoun reacted more from instinct than planning. His other hand had closed on the chair as it hit him, and now he grabbed it with both, met Doyle's smash with it in mid-air. The two chairs jarred, breaking, but it had checked Doyle for a moment, and there remained a long club of the chair in Calhoun's grip. He stabbed forward lungingly with it, and caught Doyle in the stomach, sending him back, doubled up with pain and gasping for breath.

Shaking his head, Calhoun charged, lifting the club. His swing caught a hanging lamp instead, which in his half blinded condition he had not seen, and broken glass and coal oil showered down upon him, and the force of the swing almost numbed the hand which held the club. It gave Doyle a moment to recover, and that was all he needed. He reached a bottle, set out on the bar, closed his fingers around the neck and hurled it viciously.

Calhoun dodged, and saw it hit one of the bystanders; the man dropped as if pole-axed and was dragged out of the way by one of the others. They were watching, appalled at the pace and ferocity of the battle; and now, his wind back, Doyle came charging in again, snatching up a third chair.

Calhoun ducked away from the devastating sweep of it, scrounging down, and it hit the edge of the bar above him and shattered, as he dove for Doyle's feet and caught his legs and swept him down.

Doyle hit the floor hard, and twisted, kicking. His spur raked Calhoun's ankle, but the heavy boot protected it. Doyle lunged back, reaching blindly for a weapon, and Calhoun swung the club which he still clutched, and which made a heavy, solid thud as it caught Doyle on the arm.

That arm dropped to his side as he staggered up, and Calhoun knew that it was broken. But Doyle was merely enraged by the setback. There was a table in the way now, and he picked it up with his good hand and held it, got his foot behind

66

it, then kicked, sending it hurtling at Calhoun, a devastating weapon. It caught him and knocked him off his feet, but a bottle that had been on it slid and rolled, and he caught it and threw it at the advancing killer. It missed Doyle and splintered among the other rows of bottles on a shelf behind the bar. And then Doyle was leaping at him with both feet.

Calhoun was nearly winded. The fight had not lasted long, but for sheer savagery he had never know anything like it. Doyle had taken enough punishment to put most men out, and it seemed only to have whetted his appetite. Most gunmen were no good with their hands, but Doyle was proving the exception. Calhoun managed to roll, and Doyle's jump missed him. He came up under a table, upset it in Doyle's way, and gained his feet again, and for a moment they eyed each other warily, breathing heavily.

Wreckage was spreading across the room; most of the bystanders had made good their escape. The bartender, desperate, ducked down behind the bar and came up with a sawed-off shotgun, and bawled a warning at them as he started to raise it.

But there was more than brag and treachery to Doyle. He possessed a lot of ability at this sort of fight, and the bellow of the bartender was a mistake.

Without even turning his head to look, Doyle gave a cat-like backward jump which brought him in reach of the startled drink dispenser, and his right hand swept out and jerked the gun away before the man knew what was going on. He swung it to his shoulder, holding it a little awkwardly, jerking around, and his finger was closing on the trigger as the muzzle centered on Calhoun.

6

There had been tables ranging all about the room when the fight began. Most of them had been tipped or smashed now, and the room was a shambles. But there was still one upright behind Calhoun, with a tall brown beer bottle on it. Calhoun's fingers swept it up and he flung it, and Doyle jerked a little to avoid it. The blast of the shotgun went wide, shattering a mirror. Before he could steady himself to use the second barrel, Calhoun was on top of him.

Doyle swung the gun as a club, in a savage chopping motion, and the smell of burnt powder made a heavy reek on the air, as the black powder lifted in a heavy film of smoke. Calhoun ducked back, but by now his opponent had let the gun slide in his fingers so that he clutched the end of the barrels, and he swung again, wild with viciousness like that of a charging grizzly.

That was his trouble. For the moment, between rage and pain, he had lost his head. Calhoun, on the other hand, was collected now, cool and wary. Timing himself, he ducked under the sweep of the gun, came up before Doyle could recover from the expended energy of that swing, and hit him, for the first time, full on the chin, with his fist. Behind the blow, Calhoun put all the weight he had, all the rage that was still in him.

It rocked Doyle back, but he was like a grizzly in other ways. One was an ability to absorb punishment and come on. He clung to the gun with a blind stubbornness, steadying himself with it as with a cane. And as Calhoun tried to hit him again, he lashed out with his boot, and this time it connected.

Calhoun was aware of heavy biting pain in his stomach, for the need of air where it had been sucked away from him, leaving an agony-filled vacuum. He was down, rolling on the floor, and now, with a sort of slow deliberateness, more terrible because of that, Doyle moved and stood above him and once more raised the clubbed gun for a finishing smash.

It seemed impossible to find strength in his racked frame for what had to be done. But with some hidden reserve Calhoun found it, and rolled a little, and the gun-stock grazed his skull and splintered on the floor. He reached up then and got a grip on the man, dragged him down relentlessly, shifted his hold and got a grip on Doyle's throat and brought him to his knees. And having gotten a hold, Calhoun clung with a bulldog tenacity, knowing that it was that or die, for he was still groggy and sick from the kick.

Doyle's one good fist was beating at him, he was kicking and struggling, but Calhoun kept his head down and hung fast. He tightened his fingers with a sort of savage pleasure as strength began to flow back into him and the tide of agony ebbed before it. As his head cleared, he realized that Doyle had ceased to struggle, that he had gone limp in his hands, his face purpling.

Slowly, wearily, Calhoun let go and got to his feet. There was a strange stillness in the saloon, and looking around, he saw that it was empty, though a head bobbed in a startled way from over by the door as he turned. He walked toward it on legs which would barely hold him up, and catching a glimpse of himself in what remained of the mirror, he was shocked at the sight.

Behind him, Doyle lay unmoving. Whether he was dead or not, Calhoun did not know, nor much care. Even the capacity for rage and hate had been washed out of him for the moment. His fingers touched his waist and encountered emptiness, and then he remembered his gun and belt, found them, and buckled the belt into place again.

He stepped out into the sunshine, and was aware of other men who stared at him as at a ghost, and scuttled away, but he did not pay much attention to them. The sharp sunshine hit his eyes like a slap, after the murky dimness of the saloon's interior. It reflected dazzlingly from water in a trough across the street, and he remembered pumping water there the day before, for his own horse. Somehow that seemed a very long time ago. He crossed to it now, sank on his knees, and dipped his head in the water.

When he stood up again, with some of the blood and grime washed away, he felt better. His head was clear again, and he remembered his original purpose, to go to Mrs. Abernathy's house and inquire about Harkness' daughter.

But he was in no mood to go there now, and in no fit shape. Despite his crude ablutions at the watering trough, he still looked wild and anything but presentable. And across the street now were tied a couple of horses, in front of the Sage Hotel. One bore the Wagon Wheel brand, the other the Flying A. The Three were gathering like vultures for the feast. Deliberately, he turned and trudged across the street.

Abelard Vick had been the first to arrive. He was a big man, but surprisingly graceful and light on his feet, and he moved with an arrogance which was voiced in every line of him as in every word he spoke. Even his most casual words rang with it, for it was in every one, every inflection of voice.

It was not so much conceit with Vick, in the ordinary sense of the word, as a profound conviction that he knew best—best for himself and for everyone else. And what was best for him was naturally best for others. That was the philosophy of the man, a sort of unshakable conviction in his own rightness which could see no wrong.

He had been there ten minutes when Abel, of the Flying A, came in, and had looked at his heavy gold watch three times in those ten minutes. The fact that he was a quarter of an hour early did

73

nothing to temper Vick's impatience. He disliked to be kept waiting, and it was always, as a matter of course, the other fellow's fault. He swung on Abel with a scowl.

"I've been waitin' ten minutes! And I'm a busy man!"

Abel was a short, pudgy man, with a mottled, vulpine face. An ugly customer, as more than one man had discovered in the past. But he was afraid of Vick, and he knew his temper, so the outburst was not unexpected. He looked around and found the right answer.

"I don't see Harkness yet," he said.

"He ought to be here," Vick growled. "We've work to do! Or at least I have!"

"Likely he's visitin' his daughter," Abel suggested, finding Vick's mood even worse than he had expected.

"Bah!" Vick swung sharply about from glaring out the window. "He'd better keep a tight check rein on that girl! The way she rides all around the country, all by herself, no wonder she got into trouble! The wonder to me is that she ain't done it long before—"

He checked, but did not lower his voice, as the door opened again and Tom Harkness stood there. Harkness of the Window Sash was an older man than either of his compatriots, and grown a little heavy with years. Just now his face was lined and tired, and his heavy, hooded eyes were troubled. He nodded shortly, offering no greeting or apology, and sank into a chair.

"You're late," Vick accused him promptly. "I been waitin' a quarter of an hour—"

"It's not my fault if you were early," Harkness countered sharply. "I'm right on time."

"You knew I was here," Vick growled, as though that made all the difference. It was Abel who intervened now.

"How's your girl comin', Tom?" he asked. "Better, I hope?"

"She's doing fine, thanks," Harkness said, still heavily. He looked at them from under those bushy eyebrows, and his voice held an unexpected quality of humbleness.

"My God, when I think what might have happened to her—if she hadn't been found—"

"I've told you before that you're a fool," Vick said bluntly, "lettin' her ride around by herself. You see what happens—"

Harkness stopped him, interrupting with an equally blunt impatience.

"Don't babble like a blatherskite," he said. "Such an accident wouldn't happen that way again in a lifetime. And it might happen to any of us just as well. As well tell her to stop walking, since she might fall downstairs at home and hurt herself!"

"She's your daughter," Vick said shortly, not liking the rebuff. "Anyway, we're here for important business. You both know what this meeting's about."

"Sure," Abel agreed.

"Well, I guess you've heard the news—about here in town yesterday," Vick went on. "The only trouble was, that damn stranger didn't turn out to be this new foreman after all. Seems like Calhoun had got off the stage—"

"Calhoun?" Harkness interjected sharply. "That's the fellow who helped Shirley!"

"Did you just find that out?" Vick demanded. "What's that got to do with it? I aimed to make sure he didn't arrive, but like I said—"

"Calhoun," Harkness repeated, as if the knowledge had shocked him. "Then he's this new foreman of Lone Pine?"

"Sure he is," Vick agreed, and his voice sharpened as he repeated his question. "What's that got to do with it? When it comes to business, there can't nothing be allowed to interfere—"

"And you tried to have him murdered yesterday?" Harkness persisted. His tone was edgy. "Who gave you the right to do that?"

"Who gave me the right? Hell's bells, when does a man have to have a right to fight a war? Ain't we all.in this? Or didn't you think there'd be any war, when we started to take over Lone Pine? What I was aimin' to do was try and see that there wasn't any war, by nippin' it in the bud."

"And you started out by havin' Doyle murder a man—an innocent man," Harkness growled. "And it might have been Calhoun—"

"It should have been, by rights," Vick pointed out. "If it had been, he wouldn't have helped your girl none, because he wouldn't have been there in the first place. That was just pure accident. Now what I want to know is, are you going soft on us because he did happen along by chance? Or are you in this like you had agreed on in the first place?"

Harkness looked at him, a little puzzled in his own mind. He had been a ruthless man, years before—the Window Sash had not been built up to its present pre-eminence by chance.

And he had gone into this deal of setting a deadline and working with Vick and Abel with his eyes open. But he hadn't quite liked the thing from the beginning. He must be getting old, he thought to himself. A lot of things looked different to him now from the way they had formerly.

Maybe it was on account of Shirley, and the fact that Marjorie Johnson was owner of Lone Pine. The two girls had never been very good friends, at least not close ones. But he knew, and had known from the start, that Shirley would sharply disapprove of any attempt to do Marjorie out of her inheritance.

So he had said nothing, following his policy that running a ranch was not a woman's business in any case. Vick had sided him. Running Lone Pine was no business for a woman, he had pointed out, adding that, later on, he'd marry Marjorie and she'd still have part of Lone Pine and a bigger ranch than before.

Harkness had allowed himself to be persuaded, partly because it had seemed inevitable to him that Lone Pine was to be dismembered and swallowed up, and if that was so, then a part should go to him. His neighbors, Vick and Abel, were plenty big already, without allowing them to become unduly swollen. Since the thing was to happen, he'd have his share.

He had made the agreement without quite liking it. Now he was more confused than ever.

"Maybe you're right," he agreed. "Likely it was

an accident, his comin' along that way. But he saved her life."

"Which was a lucky break for him, and her," Vick pointed out. "His being there, I mean, instead of on the stage. But don't forget—we're in this already. We've set the deadline, time an' place." He leaned forward in his chair, lowered his voice a little.

"And what I mean, we're really in. I been doing things. We warned Ogg to get out of the country. He seemed to be ready to move. Fact is, Doyle rode across today to have a look, and Ogg had started to load his stuff on his wagon. But he changed his mind, for some reason or other. So now he won't be pullin' out."

The two looked at him, not quite understanding.

"Won't be pulling out?" Abel repeated. "You mean—?"

"Somebody'll find him and bury him," Vick said lightly. "That'll give him some of the ground he wanted, permanent."

Harkness heaved out of his chair.

"You mean that Doyle murdered him, as he murdered that other stranger yesterday—"

"Murder is a word I don't like," Vick rasped. "Quit usin' it!"

"I'll use whatever word I damn please," Harkness shouted. "And that was murder!" He glared, breathing heavily, and it was Abel who intervened again as peacemaker.

"Let's not fight among ourselves," he pleaded. "After all, we knew there'd likely be trouble—and we're in it now—"

"Maybe we are and maybe we ain't," Harkness grunted. "I sure don't like the way Vick's tryin' to run things. If we're in it, we got some say, too."

"Sure you have," Vick agreed conciliatingly, a little frightened at Harkness' reaction. "That's why we're here to talk it over—to plan things together. You ain't going to let sentiment ruin everything now—after we've started things—just because of what Calhoun done, are you?"

Harkness stared at him a long moment, scowling. Then he shook his head.

"He saved her life," he said. "And Shirley's worth more to me than all the ranches in this whole country! I'll have to think that over a spell. Right now, I'm going back and see how she's getting along again."

He strode to the door and out. The two looked at each other a little uncertainly. A slow, silent minute passed, while Vick's scowl deepened. Then there were footsteps outside.

"He's back," Vick said. "I knew he would be."

The door opened. But it was Calhoun who stood there.

7

For a moment Vick stared, taken completely off-guard. His jaw went slack, as much because of Calhoun's disheveled appearance as because of the suddenness of his appearance. He had never seen Calhoun before, but from the description, he knew instantly that it was the new foreman of Lone Pine who stood before them, knew that he was in a truculent mood.

"I heard that there was to be a little meeting to decide about Lone Pine," Calhoun said softly, and kicked the door shut behind him. "So, since I'm foreman of Lone Pine, I thought I'd better sit in on that meetin'."

He came forward, smiling a little, and that smile, in view of the slow ooze of blood still trickling down one side of his face from the cut, and his whole appearance, was more terrible than the most ferocious scowl. He sank into a chair, using it as a stool, legs on either side of it, leaning slightly across the back of it to look at them. Vick found his voice, though his tongue was still a little bit thick.

"You—you're Calhoun?"

"I'm Calhoun," he agreed. "And you're Abelard Vick, I take it. And this other fellow will be Abel, eh? I thought there was three of you."

"Harkness ain't here right now," Abel croaked, and would have said more, except for Vick's venomous glance.

"We'll do to talk to," Vick said. He had recovered himself by now, was beginning to savor the possibilities of the situation. "And I been wantin' to talk to you."

"If you aim to repeat the same advice that your tough hand Doyle tried to give me, better save your breath," Calhoun advised tightly. "He'll know better—next time."

The two eyed him sharply, taking fresh note of

the fact that he had been in a fight of more than ordinary violence. Calhoun nodded.

"He didn't have his gun along," he said. "I'm not sure about that next time. Maybe he's still alive—maybe not."

They continued to stare, amazement growing in them. Both men were fully aware of Doyle's ability in a rough and tumble. He was a man who preferred his guns, but by some odd quirk, since few gunmen ever used their fists, Doyle was also known as the dirtiest, deadliest fighter who had ever come to Sage. This whole thing savored of the incredible.

"As for Lone Pine," Calhoun went on, as they remained silent, "I just wanted to tell you that a deadline works two ways. Any man that crosses Cayuse Creek from now on, lookin' for trouble, is going to find it. And if you start things, you'll find you're on the wrong side of deadline. I won't have any compunctions, once you push me, about coming across Cayuse and killing a few skunks."

He stood up then, lifting the chair back out away from him as he did so, and backed to the door. Vick was trying to find words, and finding them curiously lacking for the moment. Calhoun lifted a hand and swiped away some of the fresh blood which was running into his eye again.

"Don't say I didn't warn you," he said, and went out, closing the door behind him. It was not until the echo of his footsteps had died away that Vick began to swear, in a choked sort of way which betokened his rage and incredulity.

Calhoun felt better now. Two murders, two dead men with whom he had been, even if indirectly, involved, and for whom he felt a sense of responsibility, had been like a goad in his mind. This whole set-up of deadline, of stealing land from a supposedly helpless woman, was incredibly vicious. He had needed the release of action, and now he was in fine fettle.

He felt nearly normal, physically. Having bearded Abel and Vick in their own den had been a tonic. He thought briefly of Shirley Harkness, but he wasn't in fit shape to go calling on a sick woman. And the fact that her father was one of the Three altered things considerably. He'd get back to Lone Pine now.

He strode along, heedless of the stares of men on the street, then checked, aware that someone was calling him. He looked around, and saw that it was the medico to whom he had turned Shirley over the day before, and who was hurrying, a little breathless, to catch up with him.

"Are you going to a fire?" Fenton demanded smilingly; then his eyes narrowed. "You don't look as if you were running away from a fight, but— great guns, man, don't tell me you're running to another one yet? You look a sight. Here, come into my office. You can stand a bit of patching. Besides, I want to talk to you."

Calhoun hesitated, but the friendliness of the doctor was unmistakable, and that persistent trickle of blood was annoying. He followed him into the office, and the doctor at once set to work, cutting away a little hair, washing him, applying antiseptic which burnt him sharply, then bandaging the wound.

"What have you been up to, anyway?" he asked. "Run through a brick wall, or what?"

"That, as I recall it, was a chair leg," Calhoun murmured.

"A chair leg, eh? And who was on the other end of it?"

"Doyle, I think he calls himself. Double trouble, or something."

"He hasn't been in yet for patching up. Don't tell me that I won't be bothered with that chore?"

"I doubt if I killed him, if that's what you mean," Calhoun said. "I aimed to, but I'm more and more afraid that I quit too soon."

"His kind take a lot of killing," Fenton agreed. "But if you went that far and didn't, I'm wasting my time, patching you up. He's a killer—and treacherous as a blind rattler."

"I know what he's like," Calhoun nodded.

The doctor stood back and surveyed him wonderingly.

"Lucky that you do," he said. "Maybe Marjorie Johnson found herself a man who can handle the situation, after all. Though I didn't suppose it was possible."

"How's Miss Harkness?" Calhoun inquired abruptly.

"She's doing fine," the medico murmured. "You used excellent judgment."

"I thought of slashing her leg, but I didn't think it would be necessary," Calhoun explained.

"And naturally you didn't want to. I don't blame you. Though she'd have stood it, if necessary."

"She seems to have plenty of grit," Calhoun agreed. "But what the devil was she doing in that country, riding all alone? It's no place to ride if you don't have to."

"Probably she'd been visiting the old home," Fenton explained. "They used to live there, I understand, when she was a little girl, and her mother was alive. The place is deserted and going to ruin now. Tom Harkness never had any time to waste on sentiment. But I think it has memories for her."

That was probably it, Calhoun decided. He stood up, reached for his hat, then remembered that the doctor had said that he wanted to talk to him. But apparently he had lost interest, for he merely nodded now.

"I don't need to tell you to watch your step," he said. "But it's still good advice."

Calhoun went out. He got his horse, and was in the saddle when he heard his name called again. Looking around, he saw that the call came from Mrs. Abernathy's house, and that it was Shirley Harkness who was calling to him, from an open window.

She wore some sort of a dressing gown, and her hair was loose about her shoulders, and all in all she made a most appealing picture, framed there. There was color in her cheeks again, and Calhoun could see that she had made a remarkable recovery from her experience of the day before.

He reined across under the window, took off his hat, and saw that her eyes were fixed on his fresh bandage. Flushing a little self-consciously, he hastily replaced the hat again.

"I'm glad to see that you're feeling better to-day," he said.

"I'm a lot better—thanks to you, Mr. Calhoun," Shirley nodded. "Won't you come in?"

"Afraid I can't, right now."

"But I want to thank you," she persisted. "Really, I'm grateful. And how can I, if you don't give me the chance?"

"It's the doctor who deserves most of the thanks," Calhoun said. "It looks like he knew his business."

"Oh, he does," Shirley agreed. "Doctor Fenton is very good." The sullenness was gone from her face, leaving it alive and animated. "But he says that if you hadn't come along just when you did—" She shuddered a little at the recollection.

"You were in a bad spot, all right," Calhoun conceded. "But that's all past now." Then, remembering that her father was one of the Three, his old pride came back. It was all well enough for her to thank him, but she had done that now. And he wasn't going to appear to seek favors. He nodded, and at the change in his face, Shirley spoke quickly.

"Don't go yet, Mr. Calhoun! You—you're fore-man of Lone Pine, I know. And I—I wanted to tell you. I know that Dad is one of those who has set a deadline, but I—I'm going to talk to him—"

"You don't need to do it on my account," Calhoun said shortly, and swung his horse. "Lone Pine asks no favors—and gives none! Good-bye!"

8

I'm a fool, Calhoun reflected bitterly as he rode out of town. His quick flare of temper had died now. *She wanted to be friendly, to help me. Now I've made her hate me. And I've no right to think just of myself now.*

That was the trouble with his cursed pride and hot temper. Always before, when he'd never been more than a top hand, what he had done had concerned himself alone. If he made a fool of himself, no one else suffered.

But now he was foreman of Lone Pine, and that involved responsibility to others, to his employer most of all. Harkness would be a strange man indeed had he not been grateful for what Calhoun had done for his daughter. It was, of course, sheer luck, or accident, that he had happened along at the precise moment when he could render that help. But it had happened, and all luck aside, it had saved Shirley's life, had saved her from a horrible fate.

For, dazed and shocked as she had been, with the rattlers again growing ugly as she recovered enough to sit up, there was little doubt as to what would have happened if she had been left unaided. The thing was terrible to contemplate. But she knew well enough, and so must her father. Any man with any heart in him at all would be grateful.

Calhoun could have profited by that, perhaps have split Harkness off from the coalition against Lone Pine. That would have meant a lot.

But he'd muffed his chance, and offended Shirley as well, rejecting her offer of friendship and help. He'd acted like a boor—he, a Calhoun of the Old South, who had at least been raised to be a gentleman!

There was always one black sheep somewhere in every family, he reflected grimly, and he was it. A prideful, arrogant fool, without good sense, and getting worse, more crabbed, as he grew older. It did not occur to him that he would not even have thought such thoughts, a couple of days before; that there was a change in him.

But the thing was done, and he wasn't going back—not now. His thoughts were bitter as he rode, however, and he realized with a shock that it was mostly because he had insulted Shirley, had been so unnecessarily rude when she had offered friendship. She was, he guessed, a lonely girl, to whom life, despite her father's wealth, had not been too kind. He had had no business to treat her so.

Nor had he any business to think in sentimental terms, he told himself with sudden sharpness. He was a big enough fool without that. He had a job ahead of him, and the beginning he'd made hadn't made it any easier. They'd be out to smash him in earnest now, to kill him and take Lone Pine. Reviewing what had happened, it seemed to him now that just about everything he had done had been wrong.

He reached the ranch at sunset, and climbed wearily down from the saddle. It had been a trying day, and such days, when things affected a man's mind and his emotions, were far harder than days of sheer physical toil. On such days you did your work and that was all there was to it. A contented mind had a lot to do with the workings of the human body.

Sam Troupe was on the porch again, this time in his wheel-chair, and he gripped the wheels in white, veined hands and scuttled forward like a crab as Calhoun stepped up. His voice was still a little shrill, with that cackling quality, even though his words were sober enough.

"Look like you'd been through the mill—or puttin' someone else through it."

"I guess it's a little of both," Calhoun said, noting absently that the robe had fallen off Troupe's lap, and that his legs looked neither misshapen nor withered. He went on, into the house. He was of no mind to talk now, but a qualm smote him as he closed the door. The crippled man was probably lonely, and being tied to a chair would account for his waspishnes. Sometime, he'd take the time to talk a while.

The others were all in the house ahead of him, ready for supper. It was apparent that they had been ready to sit down to the table, but had seen him ride up and had waited, out of deference to his newness and his position as foreman. Eyes raked him speculatively as he took his seat, and he saw a quick concern in Marjorie's eyes. But no one commented until plates had been filled. Then he broached the subject himself.

"I tangled with Doyle in town," he explained. "He was almost as tough as he thought he was, too."

"Doyle?" Bailey repeated, with his quick, bird-like glance. He held his fork suspended a moment, and voiced the thought that seemed to be in every mind.

"Guess, judgin' by that, Vick'll be discoverin' he's took on a job for himself, tryin' to grab Lone Pine."

"We buried Ogg," Muskett said a little timidly. And looking at him, Calhoun was startled to discover an admiration very close to hero-worship in the boy's eyes. This was his tribute to any man who could tangle with the dreaded Doyle and return to tell of it.

"That's fine," Calhoun approved. He saw now that, whatever Muskett had been before—and he had a strong hunch that the boy had been under Wyss' influence—he might be won over. All that he needed was a little encouragement, a little help if it came to showdown. Once won, his loyalty could be worth a lot.

"Did you have any trouble?" he asked casually.

"Nary a bit," Muskett said a little scornfully.

"Didn't see anybody. Looks like you had a monopoly on what trouble there was," he added, in what was intended for a joke.

"It was a pleasure," Calhoun said, and grinned. He saw Glades looking at him with a little more respect. Three of this crew had good possibilities. It was Wyss, outwardly so obliging and so able a man, who left him doubtful. Still Muskett and Glades would bear watching.

"What about those critters off by Little Creek?" Glades asked suddenly, throwing the question jointly at Calhoun and Marjorie. "Seems to me they're in a bad place, if trouble breaks."

"What about them?" Calhoun asked, and Marjorie looked a little troubled.

"I intended to tell you about them this morning, but there was so much else that I forgot," she apologized. "There's about a hundred head of two-year-olds down by Little Creek. That's on the other side of Cayuse, and south. A sort of canyon-like valley, with only one entrance, and that is closed by a short fence and gate. They've been there a couple of months. It's good pasture, and has always been part of Lone Pine range."

"And it lies right up against Wagon Wheel," Glades added dryly.

"But it's on the other side of Cayuse—so it's not

beyond deadline," Mrs. Henry spoke up anxiously.

"Reckon anything that concerns Lone Pine is beyond deadline now," Bill Bailey said succinctly.

He was right there. But it had been Glades who had mentioned the cattle. That set Calhoun's mind at rest on one point. Sullen Glades might be, and he had been suspicious and resentful of a stranger coming in as foreman. But of his loyalty to Lone Pine there could be no question. He'd do to trust.

But if he had allayed fears on one score, he had roused new ones. He was perfectly right: the herd should be looked to. Lone Pine was in no shape to lose a hundred head of two-year-olds. Yet Wagon Wheel could be counted on to strike there, if they had not already done so. That had been a bad oversight, and the loss of even this one day might be costly.

"We'll go after them first thing in the morning," Calhoun said. "Get them on this side of Cayuse where we can watch 'em."

It was not until he had exhausted his bafflement and rage in profanity that Vick remembered what Calhoun had said about Doyle—that the man might even be dead. He moved quickly then, and it was easy to see which saloon was the center of attraction to a curious crowd, now that Calhoun had departed and the fray was ended. Vick crowded brusquely in, elbowing men aside, Abel at his heels. He paused for a moment, a bit startled at the wreckage, and then he saw that Doyle was not dead, but was sitting up, there on the floor, tenderly fingering his throat with his good hand and calling savagely for a drink.

The man was almost as much of a wreck as the saloon. Everything attested to the savagery of the fight, and even Vick stared, a little appalled. Doyle drank the whiskey which was fetched him, slopping a little of it, cursing, then got unsteadily to his feet and stood there, swaying. The wild anger boiling in him had been in no wise diminished by the thrashing he had taken.

"You'd better go over to the doctor, and then to the hotel and to bed," Vick advised. "You look sick."

"The hell with bed," Doyle raved. "I'm going to find that Calhoun and kill him. He can't do this to me."

"Looks like he did it," Vick commented dryly. "And right now, you're in no shape for any more. Go find the doc and get yourself fixed up. Then sleep it off."

Doyle stared down at his broken arm, and his lips twisted thinly. But he walked now without faltering, and the animal vitality in him was an amazing thing.

"I'll go get my arm patched up and put in a sling," he agreed. "The blasted thing gets in my way, this way. But it ain't my gun arm," he added significantly. "And next time, I won't be caught without a gun!"

Vick opened his mouth as if to dissuade him, thought better of it, and watched him walk away. It was seldom that Vick was rendered speechless, but he was secretly a little afraid of Doyle. Right now, he was well pleased that Doyle was working for him. And if he wanted to press what had suddenly developed into something of a personal feud between himself and the foreman of Lone Pine, Vick certainly had no objections.

Doyle walked down the street to the doctor's office. Fenton looked up sharply at the sight of him, but he made no comment as Doyle harshly ordered him to get to work. He set the arm and put it in splints, giving Doyle nothing more than a pull at a whiskey bottle while he worked. He even felt a little sorry for Doyle, for seldom had he seen a man who had absorbed so much punishment in so short a time. Aside from his arm, he'd be stiff and sore for a week.

Yet in spite of this, he was secretly glad that the

gunman had gotten what he had. Also, it was plain enough that all Doyle wanted now was a chance to get going again, to kill Calhoun. It would be better, the doctor reflected, and more of a service to humanity and society in general, if he used some sleeping powders on him, in that whiskey, and then saw to it that his patient died on his hands.

It could be done, and in the condition that Doyle was in, it would excite no suspicion, nor any disapproval in the community. Doc sighed as he fixed the arm in a sling. Because he was a medico, he had to heal them as they came, but this time he knew it was a mistake.

The only comfort to be gleaned was that this new foreman of Lone Pine was a right tough hombre himself, and having bested Doyle once, there was the chance that he could do it again. Yet, knowing Doyle, his treachery and cunning and the bitter venom in him now, the doctor wouldn't have cared to bet money on that.

Cleaned up, his arm set and in a sling so that it would not bother him too much, Doyle brushed impatiently aside the doctor's warning that it would be a lot better to go to bed and stay there for a few days, as well as much less painful.

"I can stand a little pain," he said. "And somebody else is going to get hurt, too! I ain't like some, who get licked and figure the feller that done it is a better man than them!"

That expressed his nature perfectly, Doc reflected wearily. Unforgiving, unforgetting, ruthless. A combination like Doyle was rare, but doubly dangerous on that account.

Doyle had steadied a little; the first wild flush of his rage, when he had come to amid the shambles of the saloon and found out his condition, had departed. He went to a restaurant and had supper, finding it a little awkward to do things with one hand, wincing and savage when he jarred his injured arm. But the pain of it, as he had told Doc, did not deter him for a moment from his purpose.

He had made one satisfying discovery. He could still use the fingers of his injured arm after a fashion, if he had to. To slide fresh shells into a six-gun, for instance.

It was dark when he reached the town marshal's office and recovered his guns. The marshal, who had heard all about the events of the afternoon, took one look at him and wisely refrained from comment as he handed the weapons over, but that did not save him from a cussing, even though Doyle had given up the gun earlier in the day without protest.

"If it hadn't been for you, I wouldn't be in this

shape now," Doyle said bitterly. "And I'm tellin' you right now, badge-toter—I ain't ever sheddin' these guns again when I hit town. And anybody that suggests it dies right then!"

He examined the guns briefly, wincing again at the pain of using even the fingers of his other hand. Then, satisfied, he slid the weapons into holsters, swung to the saddle and headed out of town. And he was riding, not for Wagon Wheel, but for the crossing which would take him by the most direct route across the Cayuse and deadline, to Lone Pine and the man he sought.

9

Calhoun had been wrong in supposing that Shirley Harkness would be offended by his curtness. A lonely sort of a person, as he had guessed, she was sharp of perception and keen of judgment, and she understood him, his pride and temper, better than he did himself. In addition, she was well aware that he had saved her life, and deeply grateful. And it was her habit in such a case to do something about it. It was a tradition in the family that a Harkness always paid his debts.

When Tom Harkness arrived at Mrs. Abernathy's, a few minutes later, he was fuming under his breath, more disturbed and upset than he had been for years. He had been a ruthless man, in his way. The size of the Window Sash attested to that. But even his worst enemies admitted to a rugged honesty in the man, according to his own code.

That honesty had been impugned now, his whole code violated. A more astute man than he would have perceived the course being taken by Vick— to be rid of opposition by the simple expedient of killing it off. The murder of the stranger who had arrived by stage, and been mistaken for the new foreman of Lone Pine, was grim proof.

And that was too much for Harkness. He had entered into the compact uneasily, but with the assurance from Vick that it would mean nothing except that Marjorie Johnson would have to give up a lady's privilege of being coy and make up her mind to marry Vick; that she would be mistress of a bigger ranch than ever, and better off, since she couldn't hope to run Lone Pine successfully.

The last had sounded logical, since the big ranch had been going downhill for the last couple of years. There seemed no good reason for it, but the fact was apparent for any cattleman to observe. Proof of poor management, as Vick had pointed out.

Presented in that manner, the proposition hadn't sounded bad. He had gone into the deal. But though he had now told Vick that he needed more time to think things over, Harkness' mind was pretty well made up by the time he reached Mrs. Abernathy's. Sight of Shirley, still a little excited from her interview with Calhoun, convinced him.

"Dad!" she said. "You've got to help him! He's too proud to ask you to change, as a favor for having helped me. But you've got to help him just the same!"

"I know," Harkness agreed heavily, and confessed what was troubling him. "But it's never been my policy to start on one side and then quit and go over to the other, right in the middle of a deal."

"If the deal's wrong, isn't that the right thing to do?" Shirley asked sharply.

Harkness eyed his daughter, a little surprised. Usually she was a silent, dreamy girl, much more given to playing alone, to long rides alone, than to expressing opinions; generally she was obedient, never one to challenge him or his ideas of what should be done. Something had stirred her now.

"Maybe you're right about that," he agreed. "But it still won't be square—to start one way and then turn. Too much like a traitor."

Shirley knew what he meant. In his own way, Tom Harkness was ruggedly honest. Nevertheless, she pressed her point.

"At least you don't have to help Vick," she said. "If you pull out, everybody will know then that the deal's crooked. He won't have a leg to stand on."

"That won't stop him," Harkness said.

"Well, what are you going to do?" Shirley challenged, and moved uneasily. "Oh, I wish I were a man!"

Harkness regarded her for a long moment.

"I'm right glad you aren't— and so are you," he said. He arose, a little wearily. "I've told Vick already that I couldn't see it his way. I'll make it plainer."

His mind was still not made up as to his future course of action as he went out. He wasn't going to go along with Vick, or have anything more to do with the steal of Lone Pine. What he wanted to do was to drop the whole thing right there. But he had a sneaking conviction that it wouldn't be that simple, and that was what bothered him.

He heard presently of the fight in the saloon, and of how Calhoun had licked Doyle. His spirits lifted a little at the news, for this was proof that Calhoun was a man, and Harkness never had liked

Doyle. The man was a monster, a throw-back: a sneaking coward who used a gun and shot from ambush, or faced a man without giving him any real chance. Harkness had known plenty. such, and he despised the breed.

But never before had he known a killer who was also a man of his hands, and with the physical courage to fight as savagely as Doyle did on occasion. And this was the first time that Harkness had ever heard of his being beaten in a fight, fair or otherwise.

He realized at once that Doyle would not let it go at that. Most men, fairly beaten, would be good sportsmen and accept the result. But not Doyle. Harkness knew about what his course would be, and presently, encountering Doc Fenton, he had it confirmed as if he had read a blueprint of the gunman's plan.

Fenton had not intended to say anything to anyone, least of all to one of the Three. But the thing was troubling him, and the threats of Doyle still rang in his ears. Seeing Harkness, he came to an abrupt decision. It was a gamble, but most of life was that way. And Harkness had a daughter who was alive today because of Calhoun.

"Doyle just got his horse and left town," the doctor said abruptly. "I wanted him to go to bed.

He wouldn't. Said he was going to find Calhoun and kill him."

Now the picture was complete in Harkness' mind. From a blueprint, it had emerged in all its grim clarity, like a photograph under the developer. Murder, according to the familiar pattern that Doyle had practiced more than once.

"I just thought you'd be interested," Fenton went on, probing with the words like an instrument in a gunshot wound. "Since Calhoun did what he did for Shirley, yesterday."

"Thanks for tellin' me," Harkness agreed, and indecision fell from him. "I'll go after Doyle."

"He's dangerous," Fenton warned. "Bad as those blind rattlesnakes."

"I guess I better get started," Harkness said simply, and spurred. He felt an odd relief, now he was going into action. It was so much easier when you knew what to do, and didn't have to figure a thing out.

Doyle's arm troubled him a good deal, the first few miles out of Sage. The reaction to the beating he had taken was beginning to set in, and even his animal-like vitality was feeling it. He rode more slowly, realizing that it would be better to arrive at Lone Pine after everyone was soundly asleep.

The best way, he decided, would be to leave his horse safely hidden at a little distance, and set fire to the bunk house. There were tall weeds and grass at one corner of it, now tinder-dry. As was the building itself. It would catch and burn fast.

From back in the darkness, he could pick off Calhoun as he came out into the flaring light of the blaze. It would be one of the easiest jobs he had ever done. And easy, as well, to slip away in the darkness, with the others occupied trying to prevent the fire from spreading—

No, it would be just about as easy, and better all around, to kill every man of them as they were driven out of the bunk house by the flames. That way, there would be no pursuit, no danger. And after all, Lone Pine had to be wiped out. This way would be quicker, surer than any other. Vick would approve, once it was done. And he'd have Vick where the arrogant boss of Wagon Wheel would have to accept him as an equal, a partner.

It was a dark night, with a sprinkling of yellow stars remote in a dark blue sky, and no moon. Just the sort for his purpose. With eyes cat-like to begin with, and accustomed to the night, Doyle moved as easily as by daylight. He always had enjoyed the cloak of night, and he could see things that most men would regard only as shadows or darker blurs.

There was a rabbit, for instance, crouching under that bush, its long ears pricked high in strained attention, while it sorted out the sound of his horse's hoofs from the other noises of the night and decided whether there was any menace in it or not. Doyle could almost see its nose twitch sensitively.

Beyond was a big boulder, as high as a horse and twice as wide. In the shadow of that a coyote had been lurking, having caught the scent of rabbit somewhere close at hand. It slunk away, ghost-like, on padded paws, but not before Doyle had seen it, caught the fierce reddish glint of its eyes as it turned them up toward him for an instant. And on top of the rock, looking like a part of the stone, sat a horned owl, also on the hunt for the rabbit.

The winged marauder did not stir, confident that a man on horseback offered no threat to it, serene in its belief that no other pair of eyes could rival its orbs in the dark. But Doyle again glimpsed the fierce hunting gleam of them and correctly catalogued the dark mass for what it was. This sort of thing was an old story to him.

From beyond, now, came the sound of Cayuse Creek, turbulent as always, and a breeze ruffled the trees and stirred the thin grass, fresh from the mist it had picked up at the creek. Another minute and he'd be out in it, and he'd stop and get a drink,

Doyle resolved, for he was uncommonly thirsty now—

His raking glance fixed on a darker blot ahead, by a clump of trees, something that appeared to be only a blur of darkness. But he knew at once that it had no business to be there, and speculated briefly as to whether it was a steer, a moose, or a man on horseback—and decided in the same breath that it was the latter. And then the man was riding forward, out into the middle of the road, and Harkness' voice challenged him.

"That you, Doyle?"

Doyle was surprised, and irritated. With the quick perception of a prowling cat, he read the inflection in the words, and sensed that Harkness was not here as an ally, even though he was one of the Three. Harkness' girl was alive because of Calhoun, and that made all the difference. Doyle's voice was wary as he answered:

"Yeah, it's me. What you want, Harkness?"

Harkness felt only relief. He had taken as few chances as possible, and had ridden cross-country, through brush and over bad trails, to get to the river ahead of Doyle, being perfectly certain in his own mind that Doyle would come this way. Harkness had been reasonably sure that he was ahead of the gunman, but there was always the possibility that he had been too slow, or had misjudged somewhere. Now that doubt was gone.

"I want to talk to you," he said. Since he was one of the Three, he was confident of his authority.

"You're headin' to try and kill Calhoun, according to what I heard," Harkness went on.

"What of it?" Doyle demanded with asperity. His wounded arm ached more sharply than ever; his whole body felt as if it had been beaten with a hammer. "Lone Pine has to be licked. And Calhoun has to be put out of the way first."

"Mebby so," Harkness conceded. "But we're not doing it that way. You stirred up plenty of trouble yesterday, killin' that stranger. Any more such, right now, and hell 'll be cold by comparison. So turn around and get home and to bed."

Harkness spoke with the authority he had long been accustomed to exercising, with a certain truculence of manner. It never occurred to him that Doyle, even in his present mood, would dispute him. But he had failed to reckon with the wild anger which had been smouldering in the man, which now flared instantly, burning fiercely against opposition.

"This is between Calhoun and me," Doyle growled. "Get out of my way!"

Harkness stared, startled, a little shocked. He sat

his horse, undecided, and it was that hesitation which precipitated things. To Doyle, raging as he was, it seemed that Harkness intended to block him, and he was in no mood to be stopped. His anger came to a head, and though, to Harkness, he was only a darker shadow there in the road, and not a good target, Harkness was distinct and clear to him.

Doyle jerked his gun and fired with the blinding speed for which he was famous. Harkness was taken completely by surprise. He did not even see the motion.

His own horse reared high in sudden terror, partly because of the startling blast of the gun almost in its face, partly because it sensed that the man on its back had been hit, and could smell already the rank odor of spilling blood. It reared and twisted, bucking, and the limp form of Harkness spilled out of the saddle and fell, and lay there in the road, a darker blur, as though a log had been left carelessly in the way. His horse, still terror-driven, galloped madly off down the road, head held high, reins flapping.

Doyle glanced down at his handiwork, and felt no compunction. He broke open his gun and, using his injured hand, punched out the empty shell and inserted a fresh one, proving to himself that he could do it under difficulties. The pain now was worse than it had been back in town, but he mocked at pain.

Then, a new idea occurring to him, he dismounted and picked up Harkness' gun and stuck it too in his belt. He could shoot just about as well by night as by day, and with the light of a burning building to aid, he should have little trouble. But an extra gun was just that much more insurance that no one would escape from Lone Pine alive tonight—no one, with the possible exception of its mistress, Marjorie. He might make an exception in her case.

10

Calhoun was tired, but sleep did not come easily. It was hot in the bunk house, even with the screened windows open. A sultry night. And his mind was busy with the problems which the day had presented, ranging from the hundred head of two-year-olds on the wrong side of deadline, to the greater, paramount question of how to save Lone Pine itself.

For, regardless of what Window Sash might do, and it was entirely possible that Harkness would withdraw from the combination and remain aloof now, still there were Vick and Abel. And Vick had surrounded himself with a crew of which Doyle was a good example. His men and the crew of Flying A would outnumber Lone Pine by at least four to one. Those were harsh odds, even if the men had been evenly matched.

But they were not. He himself felt capable of matching lead with Vick or Doyle or any of the others. And Bailey was a willing and loyal man, but old, and he probably never had been much good with a gun. Right now, he was close to negligible in what was to come.

Glades promised well, insofar as a good cowpuncher went. But he was slow as well as sullen, and not much good with a gun. Muskett was young and untried, and still of doubtful loyalty. Wyss was the only man of the four who struck Calhoun as of probably equal ability, in such a battle, with the average of the crews opposing them. But Wyss, he was more than ever convinced, could not be counted on when trouble broke.

If he had had a little time in which to get set—but there was no time. His clash with Doyle had used up any grace there might have been. Yet he did not regret that. It was far better to hit the enemy first and get them off-balance than to stand idly and wait for them to hit you.

He was nearly dozing off when he caught the sound of crackling flames, and a whiff of smoke drifted through the open windows. For a moment Calhoun lay perplexed, so close to being asleep that he was not sure but what he was dreaming. His eyes were wide open now, however, and then he caught a flash of crimson light from outside, and was out of his bunk in a bound.

Caution gripped him as his feet hit the floor. He moved to the window where the glow was spreading and, keeping back from it, looked out. One glance confirmed his guess. A fire had been set, and it was attaining headway with a wild rush. Already, in the space of seconds, the flames had enveloped the weeds and grass at the corner, were taking a hungry hold on the dry boards and racing to the roof. In the time since he had first smelled smoke, that one flicker of red light had grown to a glare which lit up the outside, all around the bunk house, like sunrise.

The others in the room were still asleep. Calhoun called them, and pulled on his boots. As the others came awake, he steadied them with his voice, forcing himself to a calmness he was far from feeling.

"Take it easy, boys," he adjured. "The bunk house is on fire. Looks to me like Wagon Wheel is outside, waitin' for us. Get your boots on!"

117

As he spoke, he was trying desperately to plan a way out of this. Such a blaze, and at such a time, could not be the result of accident. And if Wagon Wheel and Flying A were outside, waiting in the darkness, then they would be there for just one purpose—to murder the Lone Pine men as they were driven out by the fire, and would be lurking in the rim of darkness beyond.

He cursed himself for not foreseeing something like this and taking precautions, but he had not expected anything so brutal or drastic—certainly not at this stage of the game. And regrets were useless now. But he could think of no solution. If a score of gunmen were hidden and intent on killing them, they'd probably accomplish their purpose. For they had to get out of here or be burned to a crisp, and that in the space of minutes. And running out would, even now, expose them in the pitiless glare of the flames.

"If they're waiting for us, we're in a hot spot," he added casually. "There's just one chance that I can see. They'll be expectin' us to dash for it, one at a time, and be ready to pick us off. Here."

He snatched a blanket from a bunk, urged them together into a compact bunch, and flung it over them.

"Hang to it with one hand, your guns in the

118

other," he ordered. "Then we'll run together. We're a bigger target this way, but we'll maybe take them by surprise, and not be so easy to pick out. Get to the darkness, and then we can fight back."

No one offered any objection. In fact, no one had spoken at all up to now. Awakened, and terrifyingly, out of a sound sleep, they were all a little dazed, but cool and steady. A better crew than he'd figured at first, Calhoun reflected with a thrill of pride. Men who could be welded into a mighty good crew, if he had time and the chance.

He jerked open the door and they surged through it and ran. A gun flamed from the blackness ahead, and it seemed to Calhoun that every gun in his group was throwing lead back at the flash. Quite plainly, the hulking mass that had erupted from the doorway, and the response of several guns at once, had taken the gunman by surprise.

The bullet sent at them tore through the blanket between Calhoun and Wyss, but there was no immediate second shot. And then they had gained the darkness.

Calhoun was pleasantly surprised. It looked as if just one man had contrived this, and he knew instantly that it must be Doyle.

"It's Doyle," he said. "Hunt him down! But we'll have to save the other buildings, too."

119

There was one good thing. The bunk house was set enough apart from the other buildings so that, with no wind, the blaze should be possible to control, though already the bunk house was burning so fiercely that it would be impossible, not only to save it, but even to get anything out of it. But things could have been vastly worse.

There had been no more shots, and now, from the distance, there came the pound of hoofs, growing rapidly fainter. Glades came up, with a revolver in his left hand as well as the gun he gripped in his right.

"We didn't get him," he said grimly. "But we musta winged him. He dropped his gun, then skedaddled."

Wyss looked at the gun, his face grim.

"Not likely we winged him," he said. "Look here. One of our bullets was lucky enough to hit the barrel of this gun. See the lead, and kind of a dent, smeared along the barrel? Knocked it right out of his hand, of course, and likely numbed his hand so he couldn't shoot anyway."

That, Calhoun judged, was probably a pretty accurate picture of what had happened. They had had a lot of luck. If he had slept until the fire had gained a little more headway, they would have been driven forth in such headlong rout that the killer could have picked them off like setting ducks. The ruse of the blanket over all of them had helped, and that one lucky shot, hitting Doyle's gun, had completed the trick.

Calhoun had no doubt that the attacker was Doyle. He had not expected him to be physically able to do anything, at least for a few days, but it was a trick to be expected of the man.

Marjorie and Mrs. Henry had been aroused by the shooting, and came out. They joined with the others in forming a bucket brigade and trying to soak down the sides of the house and barn nearest to the flames, and in smothering sparks that threatened to start a new holocaust. When the bunk house had burned to ashes, Calhoun posted Glades on watch, with instructions to call Bailey for the second watch, and then they moved to rooms in the house and were soon asleep again.

Nothing more happened that night. Around the breakfast table, Calhoun called a council of war.

"We know pretty well what we're up against now," he pointed out. "We're beyond deadline, and they've shown that they won't stop at anything to be rid of us. From now on, we've got to have one man on watch all the time. It's not likely that they'll try the same thing again, but we can't afford to be caught napping. Luck is a string that can play out mighty quick, special if you depend on it alone.

"The first thing we've got to do is get those hundred head of cattle back this side of deadline. Glades and Wyss and I will go after them right away. Muskett, I want you to ride down to the crossing with us, and take a rifle. You'll stay there. See that nobody from the wrong bunch crosses to this side! There's other places that need watchin', but we'll come to them as fast as we can. Bill, you ride and see Sackett and DeMers, and see if you can persuade them to join in with us now, seein' that they're on the wrong side of deadline, too."

He paused, his face grave.

"That'll leave you and Mrs. Henry alone here, Marjorie. But I figure you know how to use guns if you have to. And I don't think there'll be any trouble. I don't like for some men to be alone, but we've no choice today. Bill, try and make Sackett and DeMers see that their only chance, after what happened to Ogg, is to fight. He was tryin' to run, and he got killed just the same. And if they see it, our best chance is to combine in one big crew and work together. *Make them see it!*"

"I'll sure talk turkey," Bailey agreed.

"Have any of you got any suggestions?" Calhoun asked. "If so, we want to hear them."

"Reckon you've got the best program for a starter," Glades pronounced, and there was neither sullenness nor suspicion in his eyes now.

The others nodded. They parted, and Calhoun rode with his men toward the crossing. Muskett left them there, taking a stand behind a clump of boulders, where a grove of choke-cherries lent shade and additional cover. The boy's face was serious with his responsibility now.

"There's just one thing, Mr. Calhoun," he suggested diffidently. "Up-creek about a mile and a half, there's a spot that looks unlikely—but men can get across there, with horses. I know."

That was where Doyle had crossed and re-crossed the day before, after killing Ogg. Calhoun looked at him sharply.

"Too bad you can't be in two places at once, Schuyler," he said. "But it's up to you to do the best you can till we get back."

With that, they rode on, crossing the Cayuse, then swinging south. It took an hour and a half of lively riding to bring them to the canyon where the cattle were being held, and Calhoun knew, by the same token, that it would be all of mid-afternoon before they could get the herd back to the crossing, even by hustling them along. For the better part of a day they would be on the wrong side of deadline.

Reaching the canyon, Calhoun saw why it had been used for summer pasture. The high, rocky slopes on either side made perfect walls, with evergreens and brush masking them, but not spoiling their effectiveness as a fence. In between, to a width of half a mile or more, was lots of grass, and at the far end, a couple of miles down, as Wyss explained, the Cayuse formed a barrier. There were trees and springs and lots of grass in between, and only a short fence at this end.

In the old days, when Marjorie's father had been alive and Lone Pine an outfit to reckon with, no one had bothered when cattle were pastured here. This, though detached from the rest of the land and adjacent to Wagon Wheel, was still a part of Lone Pine, and that had been that.

Now it would be different. This would be too tempting a plum to be left long ungathered. And if the cattle were still here, Calhoun knew that that would be another stroke of luck. It was certain that they would not be, much longer.

Ahead of them now was the fence, half hidden by rose briars, jutting up against the cliffs on either side. It was old, weathered, a stake and rider, with a couple of barbed wires in addition. Glades pointed silently.

The gate, of barbed wires with pickets in between, was wide open.

They exchanged glances and rode on. That might mean that the cattle were already gone—it might mean almost anything. What they had to do was to find out.

They jogged through the open gate, through grass nearly knee-high, on for a quarter of a mile. Even inside the field, the grass brushed their stirrups. Calhoun, remembering the barrenness of the prairie country through which he had crossed to get here, was still surprised that there should be such a perfect bit of earthly paradise in this spot. For that was what it amounted to. In this little valley, shut off, remote from the world, there was everything. Grass, brush, trees, water, shelter, and all the natural beauty of the unmarred wilderness.

"There's a little lake 'bout a mile from here," Glades said unexpectedly. "And talk about trout! I been wantin' to get a few days to come camp by it."

Calhoun could picture it. And the words were revealing. He liked Glades better as he came to know him. But there would be no fishing for any of them, at least for a while. Now there was grim business ahead.

Dead ahead. They rounded a bend, and saw the cattle—already rounded up, being driven toward them. And behind them were ten men—ten to three. And all ten, as the brands on their horses showed, were from Wagon Wheel. Vick himself was with them, personally directing the operation.

11

Calhoun was not much surprised. Had he been in Vick's place, he would have done the same thing, and he had been expecting something of the sort.

"Well, I'll be—" said Glades, and closed his mouth on the thought. "What do we do now?" he asked.

"Take over," Calhoun retorted briefly. "After all, they're our cattle."

Glades eyed him briefly, with a sort of wintry mixture of admiration and bewilderment in his eyes. He too was thinking of the odds, and perhaps thinking, as was Calhoun, that they might get worse. In a crisis, Wyss might go over openly to the other side. Even if he did not, and was still a traitor, it would be as bad, or worse.

Calhoun had considered that angle of it when choosing Wyss to come along with them, and his choice had been deliberate. If the man was a traitor, the sooner they found it out, the better. And if there was trouble, Calhoun preferred to have him under his own eye.

The Wagon Wheel crew had halted involuntarily at sight of them, a little surprised, then had continued to drive forward confidently. Calhoun did not slacken his pace. They came up, and Vick swung ahead to meet them, with three of his men at heel, and the others all close at hand. Calhoun got in the first word.

"I see you've rounded up our herd for us," he said. "We'll take over now."

The cool effrontery of it seemed to stagger Vick a little. They stopped, with not much space between, and Vick lounged insolently in the saddle.

"So you think we're doing this just to oblige you, eh?" he asked.

"Oblige isn't quite the word I'd pick," Calhoun said coolly. "But you don't mean to say that you've gone in for rustlin', do you?"

Vick's neck cords swelled, and his face reddened like the wattles of a turkey gobbler.

"Somebody needs to trim that comb of yours," he growled. "And it's likely to happen right soon! These critters are mavericks, open to any man that cares to put an iron on 'em!"

"Yeah?" Calhoun's tone matched Vick's for insolence. "Somethin' wrong with your eyes, way it looks. These cattle are all branded. Lone Pine."

"When an outfit's finished, the brand don't mean a thing," Vick said testily. "And Lone Pine's done."

"If you think that," Calhoun challenged, "just try puttin' a Wagon Wheel iron on Lone Pine beef. There's open season on rustlers."

He lounged there, eying Vick, and Wyss and Glades sat their horses with equal alertness, one on either side of him. Most of the Wagon Wheel had closed in around them now, plainly itching for the trouble which they felt was imminent. Unexpectedly, Wyss spoke.

"I don't see Doyle with you," he said. "I thought he was one of your crew."

Vick looked at him, suspicious, a little uncertain.

"We've got enough men here for this job," he said meaningly.

"Yeah? Well, Doyle came over and set fire to our bunk house last night—aimed to roast us alive, or kill us as we came out. As luck had it, he didn't quite do either. But we don't like that way of doing things, Vick."

Calhoun listened, his interest quickening. It seemed to him that there was a double meaning here, which Vick understood well enough. As Vick eyed Wyss uncertainly, a little of the truculence and bluster went out of him.

"If Doyle did anything like that, he did it on his own hook," Vick said.

"Maybe," Wyss agreed. "But I sure don't approve of that way of doing business."

No one had made any hostile move, but Calhoun's hand was not far from his gun. And he was making it perfectly clear that he was not watching the others, that it was Vick on whom his attention was concentrated. And Vick remembered uneasily the way this man had handled Doyle.

"We came here after our cattle," Calhoun added now. "Not after trouble. But it's up to you, Vick. If you start something, you'll not live to finish it!"

There was a long, slow moment, which passed on heavy feet. Vick opened his mouth to retort, but for once he could find no words. There was death in this man, and he could sense it as a bird senses coming storm. If trouble started, his own crew would wipe out this trio from Lone Pine—he shot a nervous, angry glance at the unmoving Wyss—yes, whatever happened, Calhoun and Glades would die.

But, and he knew this with equal sureness, Calhoun would get him first. He debated matching gun-speed with the foreman of Lone Pine, and there was a raw dryness in the roof of his mouth at the thought. There would be no victory in the death of two or three men if he was not alive to see it.

Calhoun waited, knowing the thoughts that were in Vick's mind, watching him carefully. There was always the chance that, arrogant and headlong as he was, and goaded in front of his own men, Vick would take the chance. But Wyss had made him doubtful.

It was not lack of courage which held Vick back now. The man had plenty of it. But doubt, and a virtual certainty of death, restrained him.

Vick eyed Calhoun sullenly, and looked at Wyss, and there was nothing in the ex-foreman's face to tell him anything. Abruptly, jerkily, Vick nodded.

"Reckon mebby you're right, long as Lone Pine does exist," he conceded. "And I do things accordin' to the law—that's my way, and there's

131

plenty of time. A few days don't count. If you want to get the cattle out of here, that saves us the trouble. I'm aimin' to turn a bunch of my own beef in here tomorrow."

Now he was calling Calhoun's bluff, to try and divert attention from his own back-down; and whereas Vick had been helpless a moment before, Calhoun was forced to swallow it now. There was nothing that he could do about it.

"Guess you can do that—for the present, Vick," he granted. "Later on, you'll have to get 'em out again."

"Hell 'll be cold before that time comes," Vick said tauntingly. "Well, come on, boys. We got plenty work to do that's much more important than this."

He gestured to them, led them away at a trot toward the open gate. Calhoun watched them go, troubled. He had won the round, and that was a relief. But it was clear enough that Vick had given in partly because he had gotten a new idea. Now he would be up to fresh devilment.

And he knew that Calhoun could do nothing about it. All three of them had to remain with the herd and push it along. Well, he had made his disposition of his crew, Calhoun reflected, and for the moment, that was all that he could do.

Vick was chuckling to himself as they rounded the bend and drew out of sight of the cattle, toward the gate. His men, who had been a little doubtful about his seeming to back down before Calhoun's bluff, relaxed. When the boss laughed, there was trouble in the wind, and some unpleasantness for someone.

"He thinks he's bluffed us," Vick said, grinning wolfishly at them. "Let him keep right on thinkin' so, if it amuses him! That bunch of critters 'll keep all three of 'em busy for the rest of the day. And that leaves Lone Pine wide open for a visit! Time he gets there, we'll have Lone Pine!"

He saw, from their reaction, that he had won them perfectly to his way of thinking, and it was easy to forget, even to deny to himself, that fear which had motivated him, a fear that had been a hot, bitter taste in his mouth, which had constricted his throat and seemed at the same time to lodge like a lump of lead deep in his stomach. He'd outsmarted Calhoun at his own game, and that bunch of cattle would still be his at day's end. He was playing this right, all the way.

But when his crew headed, of their own accord, toward the crossing of the Cayuse, Vick stopped them with a word.

"Not that way," he said. "There's a pretty good

chance that Calhoun's posted somebody across the creek to watch it. And in that case, one man could make plenty of trouble for us, in water like that. There's another crossin' upstream—most people don't know of it. We'll use that."

Again, he saw, he had impressed his men with his sagacity and cleverness. Any loss of prestige suffered when Calhoun had challenged him was more than recovered now. None of them had known of this other crossing.

So far as Vick was aware, only Doyle and himself knew its secret. He scowled at the thought. Doyle had been up to more devilment, it seemed, and apparently it hadn't turned out too well. The man was too much inclined to fancy himself, to do as he pleased.

Not that it mattered, particularly, this time. For Vick would have this whole job finished before night, by himself, and it would be a satisfaction to show the gunman that he could do things without his help.

Muskett, left behind at the crossing, waited impatiently. It looked to him as though Calhoun had left him here either because he figured that he was too young to be planted where there might be trouble, or because the boss didn't trust him. That

thought was bitter. He had come to have a bound-
less admiration for the cool, hard-hitting foreman,
and he wanted to ride with him, to please him.

His impatience increased as the day wore on. If
there was any trouble, it was sure to come, he rea-
soned, where Calhoun was. Taking the cattle from
the canyon might not be too difficult, though there
was more than an even chance that Wagon Wheel
would be there ahead of them. But even if they
got them started, they were almost sure to be
seen—and stopped, before they could get back to
the crossing.

Finally, inactivity got the better of him. He
had to be doing something, to get in on the fight if
there was one. He went to his horse and swung into
the saddle, and paid one last cursory tribute to duty.
He rode to a high point of ground for a look around,
and saw nothing. He was about to give his cayuse
the rein and head back for the creek and across it
when something caught his eye.

It was a horseman, off across the creek half a
mile away. Barely visible, for just an instant, between two clumps of trees. While he looked, he saw
more horsemen crossing the gap like ghost riders.
Two together, then three, then two more in single
file. That made eight in all, and there might have
been more.

His breath quickened in painful excitement. Those horsemen, unless he was badly fooled, were heading for the upper, secret crossing. Muskett had seen it used, and he was confident that he was one of the few who knew of its existence. But he was certain that Wagon Wheel knew of it.

He hesitated for a moment, torn now by indecision. He remembered belatedly that Calhoun had posted him here. But he had been ready to desert his post, anyway, and Calhoun had told him that it was up to him. Up there was where he was needed now.

Muskett rode hard, circling, keeping back out of sight of the horsemen on the far side of the stream. If they did try to cross there, he'd give them a surprise party.

Excitement was pounding in his veins when he reached the spot he had in mind and, leaving his horse back out of sight, went on foot to a point above the creek, where a big rock offered good cover. The Cayuse was a hundred feet wide here, swift and turbulent as ever, but a man on horseback could get across. And on the far bank, some distance above, since the current would carry them down considerably in crossing, he saw ten men—Vick at their head.

They were getting ready to cross. Vick was already pushing his rather unwilling horse out into the water. Muskett, his hands sweaty and trembling, levered a shell into his rifle, squinted along the barrel, and fired. He purposely aimed a little wide, and the bullet made a hollow plop in the current just beside the horse's head, where it had started to swim.

Vick was startled. He had foreseen the possibility of a guard at the lower, main crossing, but had not expected any trouble up here.

His horse snorted nervously, tried to turn about, and the swift and treacherous current caught it broadside, almost causing a catastrophe. The force of the stream was tremendous. It washed across the saddle and nearly to the top of Vick's shoulders, threatening for a moment to send horse and rider alike rolling wildly.

Vick clung frantically, clutching at the saddle horn, and the horse recovered, then turned and struggled back to the shore it had just left, but two hundred feet farther down than where it had entered the current.

Vick was soaked, his hat had been lost, and worst of all, he had been badly scared. Now he was furious.

"We're going across," he growled. "Six of us in a bunch. They can't stop us. The rest of you take cover, and when you see where that hombre's shootin' from, smoke him out! Come on, now!"

There was no marked enthusiasm in the way the others followed him, for the creek was bad medicine in itself, and bullets made it an ugly hazard. Vick himself was scared, but he dared not show it. He led the way, and five of his men pushed their horses into the current and made the try.

A few moments before, Muskett's heart had been in his throat, his hands sweaty and wet. Now he was suddenly cool and steady. Let them try it, if they liked! He'd given them warning of what to expect. This time he'd shoot for keeps.

His first bullet struck a swimming horse squarely, and it thrashed violently in the current, then rolled ponderously over, full in the path of two others. Muskett was emptying his rifle at them now with methodical precision, and whether he did any further damage or not, at least it increased the confusion and consternation among the struggling horses and frightened men. For in such melee, the grip of the Cayuse was worse than bullets.

They all won back to shore again, Vick himself leading—five horses and six men. Getting out, they hastily took to cover. Bullets were spattering against the rock behind which Muskett crouched now, whining overhead, buzzing venomously, as the quartette obeyed orders and tried to smoke him out.

But they weren't doing him any harm, Muskett noted. There would be risk in sticking his head up enough to shoot back at the ten of them now, but he reloaded, watched his chance, and threw a shot where he saw a puff of smoke. A yell testified that his lead hadn't been wasted.

He waited, watching, in high good humor, well pleased with himself. He'd stopped them, and it was plain that none of them relished trying it again. And then his complacency changed to anxiety. Some of them were sneaking back, behind cover, starting downstream again, for the other crossing. Not all of them, just about half.

If he left here, half of them would get across. And if he stayed, the others would do the same. Another bullet whined at him, by way of warning that some of them were still there. He was settling down to aim slowly, carefully, in turn, when a voice from behind him seemed to freeze his blood.

"Drop that gun, kid! Drop it, or I'll have to kill you!"

Muskett turned his head, to stare into the unpleasantly smiling face and leveled revolver of Doyle, not ten feet behind him.

12

Shirley Harkness had had a good night, sleeping well. Her recovery had been faster than she had expected, quicker even than Doc Fenton had thought it could be. She was still not back to normal, but she felt so immeasurably better that it almost seemed as if she were well.

But as the morning wore on and her father did not come to see her, anxiety replaced this new feeling of well-being. She questioned Fenton, going to the doctor's office to see him.

"Father should have been in to see me the first thing this morning," she said. "But from what I can find out, he wasn't in town at all last night. Do you know anything about him?"

Fenton, reflecting on what he did know, felt a qualm of unease. He tried to put Shirley off with generalities, but she was not to be denied. Presently she wormed out of him the fact that Harkness had ridden off the evening before, with the intention of finding Doyle and ordering him not to do anything rash.

"I knew it!" Shirley exclaimed. "I asked him to give up that idea of trying to steal Lone Pine, and to help Mr. Calhoun. Do—do you think that he's had trouble with Doyle?"

"I wouldn't think Doyle would dare go against what he says," Fenton said, with a conviction he did not entirely feel. "Your father is a big man in this country, and as long as he's still supposed to be working with Doyle's employer, he ought to carry a lot of weight."

"But he isn't back," Shirley pointed out. "Something's happened."

Fenton, alarmed, tried to send her back to Mrs. Abernathy's, with instructions to keep quiet. But Shirley was accustomed to doing pretty much as she pleased. She knew that she had no business in the saddle today. Rest would be better. But rest, in her present mood, was out of the question, and she could rest more comfortably in the saddle than in a rocker, she assured herself—better in every way. Ten minutes later, she was riding out of town.

But she had not gone too hurriedly. She carried her six-gun and belt again, and she had taken the added precaution of bringing along a rifle.

She knew where she was going. To Lone Pine. She had no way of knowing definitely, but she had a strong hunch that Doyle had probably headed that way, and that her father had followed him. She had to find out.

She met a couple of Window Sash punchers, a little way out of town, and questioned them eagerly. But they had not seen their employer. Tom Harkness had not been back to the ranch during the night. They had supposed that he was still in town.

Shirley said nothing, but her apprehension was a lively thing as she rode on. Something was wrong. She knew it with a definite certainty. But, as was ever her custom, she preferred to go ahead and do things on her own, rather than to call on others, even members of the Window Sash crew, to take a hand. That might come later.

She rode with her eyes searching the roadway

142

and alert for any sign. The failure of a riderless horse to show up at the ranch was reassuring, but not too much so. If something had happened, a horse might stop to graze along the way and be a long time in coming in.

As she neared the creek, her alertness increased. She did not know exactly why, but she had a feeling that something had happened here, that this was the logical place for disaster if anything had gone wrong. And then she saw it, close to a big boulder— a spot of blood, dull red mud now, amid the dust.

Breathing quickly, she dismounted and investigated. Others had been along the road today, and had apparently failed to notice this sign. But someone had been hurt here—probably the evening before, from the look of the drying, bloody mud.

Shirley saw other sign now, as though someone had crawled on hands and knees, dragging himself, trying to get off the road back into the brush, and taking the shortest cut toward the creek. A wounded man, she remembered, always wanted water.

With a curious, dry-eyed conviction of what she would find, Shirley followed the sign. It led her for fifty feet, and there, half hidden among the tall grass which grew rank beneath the trees, she found him. Tom Harkness had revived enough to

143

crawl that far, and then, well out of sight from the road, he had been at the end of his strength. He lay now, very peacefully, and long dead.

Having made sure of that, Shirley stood up. It was clear in her mind what had happened. He had gone after Doyle, and now he was dead. That was the way things worked with Doyle. Only one man had ever dared stand up against the killer, and lived—so far—to tell of it. That had been Calhoun, the day before.

Her mind turned naturally to Calhoun. She had to have help, and the closest would be Calhoun and the Lone Pine crew, off across the Cayuse. She went back to her horse, and as she swung into the saddle, she heard again something that had been vaguely troubling her for the last half-hour—a faint, far-off sound, that had been so muted as to be indistinct before. Now it came clearer, borne on the strong wind. Gunfire, from somewhere up-stream.

She knitted her brows, but it was too far away to think much about it, and besides, there was only silence now. She pushed her horse out into the stream, and was nearly across when she looked back. Vick and four of his men were just coming into sight from upstream, and heading for this same crossing.

They were wet, disheveled, and plainly angry. Vick shouted at her, his voice lost in the swirl of the waters, but it sounded like an order to come back. Understanding came to her. They had been engaged in that shooting up above; judging by their appearance, they had been trying to get across the Cayuse at the secret crossing. Shirley knew of it, too, though no one had ever suspected that she did. It was not half so much a secret as a lot of people had believed.

The shooting meant that they had been turned back. They wanted to get over on to Lone Pine, and a guard had been at the upper crossing and had stopped them. But now they were already splashing out into the creek, intent on crossing here, and apparently confident that they could do it. And nothing was happening.

Shirley was range-bred, accustomed to fast thinking and prompt action in emergencies. This was one, and she knew which side she was on. These men had to be stopped from getting across, and it was up to her to do it.

Urging her own horse to greater speed, she rode for that same covert of rocks behind which Muskett had originally been posted. The others were already in mid-stream as she jumped down, snatching the rifle from saddle-sheath and, turning, sent a warning bullet over their heads.

Fury rose in Vick like fermenting yeast. Thwarted at the one crossing, and with victory just in his grasp, to be challenged by a girl—and a girl who should be on his side at that—was too much. He shouted something inarticulately and dug in the spurs. And the next bullet, coolly aimed, with long pent up dislike behind it, was intended for his heart.

It missed, for the simple reason that his horse stepped on a loose, round, mossy and very slippery stone, which turned under its hoof and sent it floundering. The bullet scratched across the left side of Vick's neck, down at the shoulder, stinging, drawing blood. And a third shot, close on the heels of the other two, spilled one of his men out of the saddle, with a bullet through his gun arm.

For a moment, Shirley was afraid that she would have to kill them all to turn back that charge. But Vick's horse, scrambling to its feet again, with a vividly fresh memory of gunfire in its ears, was swinging around of its own accord, and the others followed it. Reaching shore, they kept right on going until they were out of sight, spurred by more bullets which kicked sand at their feet or whistled an ominous dirge in their ears.

"That damn girl!" Vick choked. And he swore,

146

as the full realization of what this meant came to him. He had been apprehensive the day before as to what the Window Sash might do. Now there was no question. From here on out, Harkness and the Window Sash would no longer be allies, or even passively neutral. This meant that Window Sash would be fighting actively right along with Lone Pine.

He forced himself back among the trees, to consider things calmly. Nothing was working out as he had planned, and they were being held up, turned back at the creek; that was not merely humiliating, but it could seriously cripple his plans as well. A swift strike, as he had planned it that morning, might have won everything. But to be held in check now, until Calhoun came along—

"What's that?" one of his men asked curiously, and pointed. "Looks like blood."

It was. A half dried pool of mud, formed where someone had bled. Vick examined it, saw the fresh, small boot tracks of Shirley, and followed the trail. And so it was that they found Tom Harkness.

Vick stared at the still body of his former friend and ally with tightening jaw. Now he too understood what had happened, and why Doyle had not returned to Wagon Wheel the night before. After this, Doyle had been afraid too.

Vick knew a choking anger at the killer, who had dared to go this far, and a mounting apprehension as well. Doyle was dangerous, even as a hired hand. The fact that he would kill the boss of Window Sash out of hand was proof.

It was easy now to understand why Shirley had fired on them, defending the crossing. He couldn't much blame her, after this discovery. And then, as he considered all the implications of the thing, Vick's mood grew black.

Like it or not, he was doubly leagued with Doyle now, forced to adopt the same ruthless tactics. He understood that Window Sash probably did not know what had happened as yet. So if Shirley was stopped from telling—then Harkness' death could be laid to Lone Pine, and the whole situation altered. His face grew tight and ugly.

"We've got to get that girl—now!" he said.

"How?" one of his men queried, not too enthusiastically. "We've tried up above an' here— and you can't ride across in water like that, against gunfire."

"We got to find a way," Vick said stubbornly. "Somethin' 'll turn up—or we'll make it."

He thought a moment, nodded.

"The cattle," he said. "Go get three of the men up above. Leave two there. We'll leave two here, an' take six. We'll get that herd—and drive them across like we were Lone Pine punchers doing it. Wearin' their clothes and ridin' their horses."

13

Muskett, looking into the gun which Doyle held on him, felt stiff and frozen. He had awakened once, months before, with a stiff neck. Somehow it felt that same way now—as if to move, or to try to move, would bring disaster.

Behind the gun, Doyle was smiling a little—as unpleasant a smirk, it seemed to the boy, as anything he had ever beheld on a human face. There was fear in him, but worse than that was the sense that he had been caught napping, that through his own carelessness he was allowing victory to be turned into the defeat. The thing had happened already, and there seemed to be nothing that he could do about it.

Tears came to his eyes, tears of rage and humiliation. Doyle was approaching him now, coming along with a sort of gliding motion, like a big cat. He saw the tears, and the screwed up face of Muskett, and laughed—triumphantly, tauntingly.

It was a relief to Doyle to laugh, to be within reach of victory again. Things had not been going well with him for the past several hours. Nothing had worked out at the bunk house as he had planned it, and he had had no stomach for remaining in a fight against the sort of odds that had suddenly faced him.

He still had one gun, and once the numbness had left his hand, he could use it as well as ever. By that time, however, he had left the buildings, with their flare of light from the burning bunk house, well behind. And then it occurred to him that he could not go back to Wagon Wheel.

Not after killing Harkness, and bungling this other project. He had killed the boss of Window Sash cold-bloodedly, without compunction or even much thought. Reviewing the matter coolly now, he knew that he had made a bad mistake.

If he had pulled this other scheme off as he had

planned it, that would have made things all right. But as it was, he spent a bad night, between his thoughts and the pain of his wounded arm, and he stayed across Cayuse, on the far side of deadline.

That had been partly instinct, partly wariness. No one would think of looking for him over here, and something might turn up. And he was too tired to go any farther than a good hide-out, of which there were plenty on Lone Pine.

The echoing drumming of gunfire caught his attention when it came, and he moved to investigate. He came upon the scene and saw, with a brittle amusement, how the kid was holding off a whole big crew of armed men who wanted to get across, and he judged, even without a good look at them, that these men would be from Wagon Wheel.

His first impulse was to shoot Muskett and be done with it, thus making his peace with Vick. But that, he decided, would be too simple. Besides, he was beginning to resent the imputation that he was always a killer from ambush, afraid to take a man alive.

This time it would be far better to take the kid prisoner and then dominate the situation, by proving again that he could do things when others could not. Triumph and all the humiliation of the night

were blended in his harsh laugh as he approached
Muskett.

To the boy, however, the laugh was a whiplash,
taunting him with his own failure. It stung him, and
he noted then that Doyle carried his left arm in a
sling, and that, laughing and contemptuous, he had
grown a little careless.

"Toss me your gun," Doyle ordered.

Muskett obeyed, flipping it through the air. And
the next moment, while Doyle's eyes unconsciously
followed the arc of the weapon, Muskett hit him,
jumping, butting with his head like a goat. He
caught Doyle in the stomach, taking him completely
by surprise, tipping him over in a wild sprawl
which brought him down on his wounded arm and
sent a blinding swirl of pain through him, almost
paralyzing him for a moment. Before he could
recover, Muskett had wrenched the gun away from
him, using both hands.

The ease of it staggered the kid a little, for taking a gun away from Doyle was the last thing he
would have dreamed of attempting, in a sober moment. But that laugh had done it. He twisted the
gun about now, but Doyle was on his feet and running, darting back through the brush the way he
had come, sick with pain and the fear engendered of
his own helplessness.

Doyle reached his horse, and Muskett heard him escaping. But he knew that the outlaw was disarmed and temporarily harmless. And he had to stay and guard the crossing. There was a surging elation in Muskett as he thrust the newly captured gun in his belt, then stooped and recovered his own dropped weapon. At last he was a man.

Vick rode, his face impassive, his big body solid in the saddle. Twice a little of the irritation that was in him manifested itself when he spurred sharply, without cause, but otherwise he held himself in check and fought a battle, and it was cowardice which won it in the end.

It would be so much simpler merely to post his men and himself back in the trees and brush, where nature had provided excellent cover, await the coming of Calhoun and the two who rode with him, and greet them with blasting guns before they guessed that death crouched in ambush.

That way, the thing could be done quickly, surely, with no chance of failure. It was the way that Doyle would have chosen unhesitatingly. But something in Vick, that instinct of decency which he had cultivated and presented to the world as being his true self, revolted at the thought of murder in such a fashion. It was primitive and indecent.

But balanced against that was its sureness, as compared to the chance of failure, and perhaps death in turn, in an open fight. For there was not the least doubt in his mind that Calhoun would fight.

The advantages of the plan outweighed his doubts, but there was another angle to it. What would his own crew think, and do? Would they stoop to taking part in such a slaughter? Vick was inclined to think that they would, if he set the example. They were a pretty tough bunch, with most of their principles long since sold along with their guns.

But even if they followed him, Vick knew that they would despise him, even as he would despise himself. And it was that fear of their opinion and the opinion of others that caused him to reject the idea. At any rate, the odds were good—six to three, or perhaps six to two. In which case it would really be seven to two.

He was debating whether or not to tell his own men now that Wyss had long been in his pay. There were advantages and disadvantages both ways. A secret like that was useful only so long as the fewest possible number of people knew it. And a man who would take pay from both sides deserved no special consideration, in any case. If he got shot in the fray to follow—

Added to that was the fact that Vick didn't quite trust the informer. There had been some funny things happening, and a man who would betray one side might in turn betray the other. No, he'd say nothing—now.

They sighted the cattle, tired now and moving more slowly, inclined to try to slip off into the brush, to escape and go no farther if they could help it. It kept all three men busy to push them along and keep them together, and all of the trio from Lone Pine looked hot and tired. But they did not pause at sight of the six from Wagon Wheel. They came on, pushing the herd ahead of them, and Vick and his men swung to one side and let the dogies drift by.

Then, abruptly, at a signal from Vick, they had their guns in their hands and the showdown had come.

Calhoun had watched the approach of the others, and their very silence, the manner in which they rode and pulled aside, made it plain what they intended to do. Glades and Wyss had been no less certain, and the one encouraging feature was that the ten of the morning had dwindled to six now. But those odds were heavy enough.

Wyss had watched the approach with mixed emotions, uncertain as to where his loyalty lay. Then, as the guns began to blast, he saw with amazement that two of the Wagon Wheel crew had picked him as their target, and the next moment a bullet tore through his left arm, just below the shoulder, nearly unseating him, making him sick and dizzy. The bridle reins, which he had been holding with that hand, dropped as the arm went limp, his horse pitched wildly, and the next moment he was on the ground.

Now Wyss' predominating emotion was rage and outrage. The fact that he had been treacherous himself in the past, selling information; even the vital information that the title to Lone Pine was technically not good, was washed away in the face of this treachery from the man whose gold he had been taking. Wyss turned on his side, and now his good hand was clawing for his gun.

Calhoun was cool and alert. The unmistakable fact that the Wagon Wheel intended to kill them had a steadying effect on his nerves. When you knew what you were up against, you could fight it that much better. Out of the corner of his eye he saw Wyss' horse plunge away riderless, knew that the ex-foreman had been shot, and that too furnished relief and certainty. He knew now which side Wyss was on in this. Now it came down to a question of fundamentals—of survival.

That one detached side of his mind was like a spectator, able to watch and take note of things even while the rest of his energies were bent on what had to be done. It was curious how much powder could be burnt and lead expended at close range, and how relatively little of it would take effect.

A lot of the fire was being concentrated against Calhoun himself, and yet he was so far untouched. A spatter of lead had gouged a chunk of leather out of his saddle shoulders, a bullet had whined venomously close to his ear, and death stood in the stirrups and gibbered, but behind the mockery was indecision.

His own gun, he realized suddenly, was empty. Calhoun thrust it back in holster and jerked at the rifle in saddle-sheath. A long gun was not much good at such close quarters, but it was better than an empty one. He had it out, and as the curved stock cuddled against his shoulder, he fired, where one of the Wagon Wheel had galloped up and was steadying for a finishing shot at him.

The two guns seemed to blast in one great jarring concussion, and then the other horse had spun about and was running, the saddle empty, while a lock of Calhoun's own hair, close-clipped, fluttered before his eyes.

He saw the others from Wagon Wheel, in the grip of sudden panic, whirling their cayuses and running too, while Vick, trying desperately to check them, was caught in the rush and his own horse grew unmanageable and plunged along with the rest.

It was finished for the time being, not in the bloody finale that Vick had intended, but with one casualty on either side. The man from Wagon Wheel was dead, a huddled heap on the ground, his own six-gun still clutched in desperate fingers, a tiny fragment of smoke eddying up from the barrel, like the ghost of his own departed spirit.

Calhoun steadied his horse, and saw Wyss on the ground, and Glades bringing his own cayuse under control again. Glades was cursing, in a steady, excited monotone. He looked at Calhoun and stopped, and shook his head in wonder.

"All that shootin'—and we're still alive!" he said.

"We're lucky," said Calhoun, calmed his dancing horse to a walk, and rode closer to Wyss. Glades followed him.

"Guess none of them had our name on it," he said.

159

Calhoun had had one quick look at Wyss, there on the ground, had seen him twist and half rise up, thumbing his gun, and had decided that the man was not badly hurt. Now he swiftly revised that first judgment as he dismounted. Wyss was lying on his back, still and limp, as he had sprawled back, and there was blood on his arm and blood on his chest. His face had lost its florid color and turned the color of dirty snow.

Evidently he had taken a second bullet after he was down, and that one had a fatal look to it. It had torn the lungs, close above the heart, and if Wyss was still alive, that was about all.

Calhoun doubted even that, but as he bent lower, Wyss opened his eyes. They were dull with pain, clouded with something not of this earth, so that for a few moments he stared stupidly. Then they cleared a little, and he managed a hoarse whisper.

"Water!"

"I'll get some," Calhoun promised. "Take it easy, old man."

Seeing the stricken look on Glade's face as he came up, Calhoun added quietly:

"Take it easy. There's nothing much we can do for him."

There was water not far off, a small spring which bubbled out from under a big, mossy boulder and ran in a tiny undaunted course down a coulee, before reaching the open and losing itself. Calhoun dipped his hat at a little pool and returned with it. He had been pretty certain that there was no love lost between Wyss and Glades, but now Glades looked like a big boy ready to cry, and a little ashamed to be caught at it.

"I'll get them, make them pay for this!" he muttered deep in his throat. "I'll get them!"

"Don't worry," Wyss said unexpectedly. "I got what was coming to me."

He looked curiously calm, with the certain knowledge of death in his eyes, and that certainty lent him a dignity beyond anything he had ever possessed in health. Calhoun lifted him gently, and held the hat, and Wyss drank a little, and choked, then drank again, and sank back, his eyes bright.

"Thanks," he gasped. "I won't—keep you waiting here long." He looked up at Calhoun, with a curious expression in his eyes.

"You've been worried—about Muskett," he said. "Well, he's all right. He liked me."

Wyss paused for a moment, as though considering this fact for the first time, and finding some small cause for wonder in it. Then he went on.

"He was scared that I was crooked—and tryin' to keep an eye on me. And him just a kid! But he's

161

all right. I was crooked—I guess you knew it. But they double-crossed me—and I finished, fightin' for Lone Pine. I wish—you'd tell—Marjorie—"

There was more in his eyes, but now the words stuck in his throat. He coughed again, and crimson foam was on his lips, and as he lay back, Calhoun saw that he had kept his last promise: not to keep them long.

14

It had been a bad day for Vick, and contemplation of its mistakes lent added savagery to his mood. He saw the hundred head of cattle come up the trail, herded by Calhoun and Glades and swing toward the crossing, with the white water a froth ahead. And he found a certain morbid satisfaction in the knowledge that Wyss was not with them.

That could only mean that Wyss was dead, and Wyss had been working for him. But a bullet from the ex-foreman's gun had wounded one of the four men who still rode with Vick, so that by the next day, he'd have to take to his bunk, and would be of little use for the next week or so. The fact that the wounded man had bragged of shooting Wyss in turn, after he was down, didn't matter. The thing was done, and illy done from beginning to end.

Even when the herd swung toward the crossing, Vick realized that, with two men there already to watch the road, and three good men with himself, they could renew the fight and perhaps win it. But the trouble was that he no longer had three good men.

Their confidence in him had been shaken at the start, that morning, and three times they had gone into action since then and three times tasted defeat. Now they were a hang-dog outfit and there was no fight left in them. It would be useless to suggest it to them.

He watched, hopeful that the two waiting at the crossing would challenge the passage of the herd, but they had seen him and his followers, of course, and when they made no move, the pair took their cue from them and kept out of sight.

It was incredible that things could go so badly. His mistake, of course, had lain in allowing Calhoun to make him back down in the first place. That had set the pattern for the whole day, and once a pattern was established, it had a freakish way of continuing.

"One of you take Stumpy home and put him to bed," he instructed now, rousing himself. "Two of you go back and bury the others." His eyes narrowed speculatively. "And get a wagon and bring it back here for Harkness. We'll take him into town. By tomorrow things 'll be diff'rent—" A little of the old snap came back into his tone. "A damn sight diff'rent. Send the rest of the boys back here, too."

There was nothing more to do today save to catch up the frayed ends of a badly raveled plan. But he'd post guards at each crossing, two men at each place. If one man, or a girl, could hold the crossing against a crew, two men could do it that much better. Vick went to them and gave his orders in person.

"We're in control on this side of the creek," he said. "See to it that nobody gets across to this side —nobody, understand? If anybody tries it, fire a warnin' shot. If they keep on comin', shoot to kill!"

With that attended to, he felt better. His mistake had lain in being too lenient. He wouldn't repeat it. Harknes was dead. Shirley Harkness was on the other side of deadline, so she could not tell her story of what had happened to anyone on this side.

Back at home, Vick washed and ate a leisurely supper and felt better. By then, the wagon with the

165

body of Harkness had come in, and he climbed to the seat and drove it into Sage.

The evening was well advanced when he got to town, which meant that it was the liveliest hour of the twenty-four. Most men on the streets were more than a little drunk, and most of them had known and liked Harkness. In town now were the crews of the Window Sash and the Flying A. Vick had sent word to Abel to be there, had sent other word to the Window Sash that Harkness had been murdered and that he was bringing the body into town.

Beyond that, he had offered no information. Let men speculate as to just what he meant. Now he saw with satisfaction that the news had spread. Someone saw the wagon, and a crowd was waiting, under the moon, as he pulled up near the middle of town.

Vick turned then, with a fine sense of the dramatic, and lifted the canvas which had been draped across the body of Harkness. The cattleman lay on a deep bed of hay, over a blanket, and there was proper regret and reverence in Vick now.

"We found him out at the crossin' on Cayuse, leadin' to Lone Pine," he explained. "He'd got that far, and been killed when he tried to cross. They've got guards at every crossin', and say they'll kill anybody that tries to get to the other side."

166

He let it go at that, not charging directly that Lone Pine had done it. But, as he had foreseen, there was no need. Everyone knew that Harkness had leagued himself with Vick and Abel against Lone Pine, and the answer was obvious.

"What about his daughter?" someone asked. "Where is she?"

"She got nervous and rode out that way," Vick answered. "I guess she found him—and like to went crazy. She saw what had happened, quick enough, and started across Cayuse."

He waited a moment, while the suspense mounted and growls went up from the astonished onlookers. One Window Sash puncher swore.

"You don't mean to say they shot her, too?"

Vick shook his head.

"Nope. They let her come, then grabbed her when she got across. One of my men saw it. They've kidnapped her now."

Again, he was too shrewd to amplify his statement or to draw conclusions. And the wisdom of that course was at once apparent. Everyone was ready to draw the conclusion that he wanted of them. Public opinion now, including that of the crews of Flying A and Window Sash, was solidly behind him. Many cried out for action—immediate action—in retaliation against Lone Pine.

Likewise, they wanted to lead a rescue party for Shirley.

Vick listened to them, then shook his head.

"We'll do something," he promised. "But it don't pay to get too hasty. Like I say, they've got every crossing guarded. Not easy to get across, now. But we've got every crossing watched on this side, too. Sort of a double deadline.

"In the mornin', we'll bury Harkness proper. After that, we'll take this other up."

They were behind him to a man, accepting his leadership unquestioningly. Vick chuckled to himself. It hadn't been such a bad day, after all.

One man who would have disputed that opinion was Doyle. It was the worst day, counting from the hour of his encounter with Calhoun, that he had ever spent, the longest, blackest twenty-four hours that he could remember. The culmination had been when Muskett, a beardles boy, had made a fool out of him.

That was why it had happened—because Muskett was only a kid, and Doyle had given him scant respect or consideration. It would have been easy to kill Muskett from ambush, as he would have done with an older man. But because he was only a kid, Doyle had preferred to take him prisoner and turn him over to the rest of the crew.

And Muskett had caught him off-guard and had made a complete fool of him in turn. Worst of all, he had taken Doyle's last gun away from him.

With the weapon that he had taken from Harkness, Doyle had had three guns. But in the darkness, the night before, he had bumped against a tree, and his injured arm had pained like fire. He had fallen, and slid down a sharp incline, and somewhere in that descent he had lost the extra gun, and had not discovered the loss until daylight. Now he was weaponless.

Truly, it had been a bad day for him. His arm, racked and jolted repeatedly, was a solid sheet of flaming pain now, against which he was forced to clench his teeth to keep from crying aloud. Physically he had always been able to stand a lot of pain, but now it was getting him down. From that, he knew that he was in bad shape, and realized belatedly that the doctor had been right when he had told him to go to bed for a few days.

It was too late for that now. What he needed now were Fenton's ministrations again, and then rest. That meant getting back across the Cayuse, and the long, unpleasant ride into town. But the thing of immediate importance was to recross Cayuse.

He waited, with such patience as he could muster, until Muskett finally left his post. But his elation was short-lived, for almost immediately another man took his place, and this, Doyle saw, was DeMers, one of the other landowners on this side of deadline. That meant that Sackett and DeMers had come in with Lone Pine on the fight, that Calhoun was giving the orders now. He would have a good crew behind him at last.

From his hiding place, Doyle had watched the return of Calhoun and Glades with the cattle. He had known then that things had not been going too well for Vick during the day, but had been too engrossed in his own troubles to think or care much about it. Fever was burning him up, and he had to drink a lot of water to be able to think clearly at all.

Now he considered the matter. If DeMers was on guard here, it would mean that guards would be posted at this and the lower crossing all the time. There was one other crossing, miles upstream, but it would probably be guarded now too. Calhoun would not overlook that.

Which complicated things considerably. Without a gun, how was he to get by the guards? If he tried it, he would be challenged and shot.

Normally, he could stalk a man and drop on him and handle him with his hands. But in the

170

shape in which he now was, any such action was out of the question. One more jar to his burning arm and he'd be helpless.

There was a fourth crossing, but Doyle was of no mind to try it. It was guarded more effectively than any guns could do. The sands were treacherous and quick, and even a strong horse could not move fast enough to get through them and to safety on the far shore. It had been tried more than once. Some men had vanished. Others had been rescued. But ordinary quicksand was molasses in winter compared to that stuff.

So there seemed only one thing to do, and he did it with such patience as he could muster— waited while the slow moon rolled across the skies and at long last sank out of sight again, and full dark closed down. Now he could get across, eluding the guard without too much trouble.

In the meantime, the guard had been changed. DeMers had gone, and someone else was on watch. Doyle slipped his horse into the water, and breath flowed more easily into his lungs. He had gotten away unobserved. It would be easy now.

He was halfway across when a flame of crimson stabbed like a sword against the darkness of the far shore, and a bullet hummed warningly past.

Doyle cursed in sudden frantic rage. Somehow

he had overlooked the possibility that Vick would post guards on the opposite side of Cayuse, though now he realized instantly that it was the logical thing to do. That guard, alert and watching the stream to guard against such a crossing from Lone Pine,had seen him out against the dark sheen of the river, and that first bullet had been meant as a warning.

If he tried to go on, the next shot wouldn't be merely a warning. Doyle shouted hoarsely, calling out his name, that he was a friend. A second bullet spat at him, and it was so close that he knew it had been aimed to hit. The darkness had saved him, but that fellow was a good shot. If he came closer, he'd stop a bullet.

Desperately, still shouting, Doyle kept on. Again the gun cracked, and he realized with a sense of futility that the sound of the waters drowned out his voice so that his words were as indistinguishable as his figure. There was nothing to do but turn back. Either that or be killed.

And now he was caught between the horns of a double dilemma. If he turned back, the guard on this side would be interested in him, suspicious because Doyle had not come to him before starting the crossing. He had no choice, however. His horse had swung of its own accord, frenzied as the bullets came close, and it plunged wildly, slipping and sliding, sending darts of fresh agony· through his arm. Someone shouted at him, but the cayuse reached the bank, almost riding down a man who stood there, forcing him to leap back.

Another bullet, fired from this side now, narrowly missed Doyle as his horse raced into the brush, and a whipping branch lashed his broken arm and made him shriek with pain. Wild dizziness overwhelmed him, and then he was falling, clutching at the saddle horn to save himself, missing, and rolling on the ground.

He lay there for a while, until some of the agony subsided and his whirling head was better, listening to the receding sound of his running cayuse. Now he was afoot as well as without a gun—and trapped on the wrong side of deadline! And by now the guard would know who he was, and that he was on this side!

15

Shirley was waiting, there at her self-appointed post, when Calhoun and Glades crossed with the herd. Her smile was a little wan, her face white as she greeted them, and she leaned with one hand against one of the boulders to keep her knees from buckling.

"I'm glad to see you," she said. And then, despite her resolution not to do so, she keeled over in a faint.

She had kept going, up to then, on sheer willpower. The afternoon had dragged interminably, and she had early discovered that she was not so strong as she had first supposed. Illness had returned, and nausea had several times threatened to overwhelm her. She had had to fight to keep alert, but she had watched the crossing until they came.

Calhoun sprang down from his horse and rushed across to her, and a quick look around, at the empty shells on the ground, showed him why she had been waiting there and what she had been doing. He gathered her up in his arms and lifted her into the saddle, then swung up behind her.

"She's been keeping watch here, guardin' the crossing," he said to Glades. "Likely some of the Wagon Wheel are hiding across there now. You stay here till I send someone else."

Muskett had been posted on guard there, and there was no sign of him. Calhoun's thoughts were bitter as he rode toward the buildings. He'd hoped for better than that from the kid. Then he glanced down at Shirley, soft and pliant and now oddly childlike in his arms, and his face softened a little. As he did so, her eyes fluttered open, and then she strove to sit up.

"Did—did I faint?" she asked. "I would do some fool thing like that, wouldn't I?"

"You look all played out," Calhoun said. "I can see that you've been guarding the crossing—I set

Muskett to do it—but you should have stayed in town and taken it easy."

"I couldn't," Shirley explained. "I had to find Dad." Her lips trembled a little. "When I got there, they were trying to get across—Vick and his crew. So I had to try and stop them. I think that Muskett has been holding some of them off at the crossing a couple of miles upstream. I heard shooting from up that way."

Calhoun was curiously relieved. Not alone that the deadline had been well guarded, but because Muskett had come through. There was a lot of promise in the youngster.

"What's that about your father?" he asked.

"Doyle killed him," she whispered. "Last night. Right across the creek there. I found his body."

She told the story then, a little at a time, and Calhoun had it by the time they reached the house. Bailey was there, with Sackett and DeMers and all but one of their joint crews. That one had already been placed on guard at the crossing farther up-river. Bailey had been completely successful in his mission.

"Sensible thing to do's to fight together," Sackett agreed. He was a little man with a big voice which rumbled up from deep in his chest. "We sure ain't going to run like a pack of sheep when a coyote howls. Reckon we'll give 'em more of a fight than they're countin' on."

Marjorie greeted Shirley warmly, once she understood what had been happening. But there was a certain reserve between the girls, nonetheless, a sort of ancient antagonism which could not be so easily brushed away. Watching them for a moment, Calhoun found himself contrasting the two.

He had come to entertain considerable respect for his employer since coming to Lone Pine. Her choice of his former boss for a guide, and acceptance of his advice, showed that she had good sense. And the way in which she had torn up that contract and won his loyalty in doing so had been shrewd.

Yet he could see a wide difference between the two girls. Shirley was quick to act on her own initiative, to go out and do things like a man. She had demonstrated her ability along that line today.

Marjorie, on the other hand, had not been too successful in running Lone Pine. And even with all the danger that threatened it now, she spent most of her time at the house, working alongside Mrs. Henry. It simply did not occur to her to do such things in the field as Shirley did as a matter of course. She was a homebody, a natural housekeeper. That was what she was fitted for.

Home! Somehow, he had never thought much about such an idea before, and this was a queer time to get such notions, in the midst of strife. He shrugged and turned away, and his attention was further distracted by the arrival of Glades, whose relief had arrived at the creek.

Glades motioned to him with a jerk of the head; Shirley saw it and came as well.

"If it's something about Dad, I want to know," she said.

"Yeah, it is," Glades agreed. "A wagon came from the Wagon Wheel, with a couple men, and loaded him in and drove away. I could see what they was doing."

Shirley looked at Calhoun questioningly, and he pondered this a moment, and then it became clear enough to him.

"Vick will take him into town, of course," he said. "He'll make a big play about your father being his friend and ally, and say that we killed him. And they'll aim to give him a big funeral in the morning."

Shirley blinked rapidly once or twice. Glades spoke up.

"They're keepin' guards across the creek, to stop ary of us from gettin' across," he said.

"Naturally," Calhoun agreed. "They'll be saying that we killed him, and that we kidnapped you, Shirley. That way, they'll figure to turn your crew against us—and the whole country as well."

The danger was too real to be ignored. It might be possible to fight Wagon Wheel and Flying A, if public opinion was neutral, or else on their side. But if deadline was maintained and the whole country was against them, it would be a hopeless task.

"What can we do about it?" Shirley asked.

"Do you feel up to travelin' again—after a few hours sleep?"

"Of course," she agreed.

"Then we'll attend your father's funeral in the morning," he decided. "I think that'll be the best way. Get some supper now, then sleep a while. You'll need it."

Glades made no comment until she was gone. Then he shook his head.

"Sounds good," he conceded. "All but one thing. How you going to get across Cayuse? They sure won't aim to let either of you."

That was what worried Calhoun. Had it been himself alone, he would have risked the guards on the far shore, but Shirley changed things. And it was important that Shirley should be there. She, and

179

she alone, could deny the thesis which Vick was trying to establish.

There was no boat on Lone Pine, but it developed that DeMers had one, and Calhoun dispatched a couple of men to get it and move it to a designated spot by wagon. DeMers was frankly skeptical of the whole idea, however.

"You're welcome to it, and it's not a bad boat," he said. "But I long ago gave up tryin' to use it on Cayuse Creek. Sometimes use it for duck huntin' on a little lake, is all. Cayuse is too swift and treacherous for any boat. And if you try it where they see you, it'll be just as bad as with horses. Even if you get across, you'll be afoot."

"The first thing is to get across," Calhoun said. "I used to row a boat quite a bit, so I can handle it. And we'll cross where no horse could do it—in the canyon. They'll not be lookin' for us along that stretch of water."

DeMers' face lightened a little with slow approval.

"And if you get across, it ain't far across country to Window Sash, and horses," he agreed. "I hope you have a lot of luck."

He did not add the obvious thought that they would need it. Calhoun was under no delusions. Traveling on an unknown stretch of water at night, and on the Cayuse in the bargain, was risky.

But Shirley was bright-eyed and fresh when she awoke, a little after midnight, and they sat down to breakfast. Marjorie had gotten up to cook that breakfast for them, and to see them off. There was something deep and unfathomable in her eyes as she looked at Calhoun.

"I hate to see you go," she said soberly. "But the best of luck—to both of you."

The moon had set, and the night was dark, star-sprinkled, briskly cool. Shirley looked up at him as they rode, her face a pale oval under the starlight, excitement quickening in her tones.

"This seems sort of like a pilgrimage," she said. "And I guess it is, too. One to right a great wrong."

It would do her good to talk, Calhoun knew, She needed to relieve a store of pent up emotions, and to keep from thinking too much about the tragedy of the last few days. Curiously, he felt in the same mood.

"You sound a little like Sir Galahad—or was it Lancelot?" he said. "Anyway, one of those knights who wanted to do great things."

"And this is night, too, isn't it?" she said, and laughed a little, then was instantly sober again. "Do you know, you're a lot different from what most people seem to think you are. I think there's a touch

181

of the poet in you, too."

"I used to think there was," he agreed. "But that was quite a while ago."

"But you can understand such things," Shirley urged. "You can understand, I think, why I was riding to that old house, the other day. Most people think I'm kind of crazy to go there."

"It was your old home, I understand."

"Yes," she said. "And the only place where I was ever really happy. Mother was alive then—and we didn't have much. But Dad was a different man in those days—that was sort of a pilgrimage, too," she added softly.

Calhoun had the picture now of a lonely girl-hood, fed chiefly on memories, of a rebellious spirit breaking loose occasionally in the only way she knew—riding untamed broncos across the plains, climbing mountains, demonstrating to the world that she was a tomboy, which at heart she essentially was not.

They came to the boat, with the dark sheen of Cayuse just beyond. The night was very still, with not even a breath of air stirring. Only the murmur of the river, swift but deep here, came to them, and somewhere the plaintive notes of a sleepy night bird. They left their horses to be picked up later, first unsaddling. Then Calhoun shoved the boat out into the current, Shirley took her seat and he followed.

Almost at once he was aware of the pull of the current. It was the same here as where horses had to struggle to keep their footing, or suddenly find themselves swimming. There was an insistence to it, a sort of savage strength out of all proportion to the size of the stream. It was as DeMers had told him, earlier in the evening.

"If Cayuse was spread out like most streams, they'd sure call it a river—an' a good-sized one. It's penned up now like a strick of dynamite, and always tryin' to bust loose."

DeMers had advised him that this would be the best place to try to cross. It was a long section where no one was likely to be on watch against any such attempt, and the current was more favorable than at most points.

Here it was deep and swift, and would quickly carry them into a canyon. But the canyon was not a long one, and once through it, they could easily reach the other shore, with the current itself aiding them.

"Only thing you've got to watch for is to keep in mid-stream through that canyon," DeMers had warned. "I made it, twice, then got better sense. It's tricky as a five-year old steer."

Calhoun saw what he meant as the smooth, black walls closed on either side of them, so that they seemed to travel through a lane of midnight, with only the far stars overhead. Now and again the current would seem to jerk, suddenly and without warning, like an unseen hand, first this way, then that. It took all his skill and watchfulness to avert disaster, even with the assurance given him by DeMers that there were no obstructions in the stream itself.

The creek was rightly named Cayuse. Now they were rocking and plunging as if on a bucking horse. The stars leaped and dipped crazily, the surge of the black water made a roar despite its seeming smoothness. Deep down under, there must be great boulders fighting the current.

Without warning, the boat shot for one of the walls. But now they were starting to emerge, the light was strong enough so that he could see the danger. Calhoun fought it, dipping his paddle until it threatened to crack in his hands, and they ripped past the danger point with inches to spare.

Then they shot into the open. And now, having failed, the stream was suddenly sedate and tranquil, carrying them easily in to a smooth beach, with brush and trees growing down close to the water's edge. The creek itself still ran deep but more slowly, right up to the bank. He caught the outreaching limb of a tree, then held it fast and drew the boat close, holding it so that Shirley could step out. Then he started to do the same himself.

Her scream warned him, cut short off in the middle of a strangling note. He spun around from drawing the boat up, to see her struggling in the arms of a man who had one arm crooked about her neck.

With the other hand he was leveling a six-gun at Calhoun, at point-blank range. And this man was one of those who had suffered frustration at Calhoun's hands the morning before.

16

One part of Calhoun's mind gave grudging admiration to Vick's generalship. Everything depended now on his keeping Lone Pine bottled up, and Vick was overlooking no possible crossing of Cayuse, even by boat. He had placed a guard at this unlikely spot just to be on the safe side. And the man had watched them come hurtling out of the canyon and sweep inshore. All that he had had to do was to step out and grab at Shirley, and throw a gun on Calhoun.

Calhoun dropped, instinctively, and heard the

eerie whine of the bullet passing just above his head, followed, an instant later, by the disappointed bark of the gun. He knew that he would have been too slow to save himself. But Shirley, struggling furiously in the grip of her captor, had lashed out savagely, kicking him on the shins, grabbing at his hair and pulling. That had been enough to spoil his aim, and it was all that Calhoun required.

He swung around as he came to his feet again, and he still carried one of the oars in his hand. The flat of the blade caught the guard alongside his arm, and the gun flew from his hand. He let go of Shirley, cursing, clutching at his numbed elbow with his other hand. Calhoun picked up the dropped gun.

"He'll have a horse somewhere around," he said to Shirley. "See if you can find it. Then you can ride. And that was good work—pardner!"

Shirley flushed in the darkness. It wasn't so much the words as the way he had said them. She had never realized before that so much meaning could be crowded into the simple term, pardner.

An hour later, they came in sight of the buildings of Window Sash, and even in the softness of dawn it had a cold, cheerless look. There were no trees, no shrubbery or lawn, the buildings were stark and square. It was a big outfit, which had been built solely with the idea of efficiency. A place to eat and sleep, but not to live in. Harkness, after losing his wife, had concentrated on power and wealth in an effort to shut out memories of happier days.

Seeing it, Calhoun could understand how Shirley, though perhaps surrounded by such crude luxury as money could transplant to a few rooms inside, had still been desperately lonely and unhappy.

Despite the earliness of the hour, a strange quietness hung over Window Sash. Nearly everyone had headed out, some time before, for Sage and the funeral of the boss. They discovered one man left behind—Bender, the cookee, a slouching individual dolorously surveying a stack of breakfast dishes still to be washed. He swung around and stared with open mouth at sight of Shirley and Calhoun.

"Miss Shirley!" he gasped. "I—I heard tell that you'd been kidnapped!"

"And did all of you believe it?" she asked sharply. "Didn't any of you stop to think that it was Mr. Calhoun who had saved my life in the first place?"

The cookee looked a little sheepish, then grinned.

"Somethin' to that," he conceded. "On the other hand, Miss Shirley, that might be a plumb good reason, too."

Shirley colored a little. Bender took charge of their prisoner, once they had explained what had happened.

"I'll shut him down cellar," he said. "No chance of his gettin' away. I'll sure keep an eye on him. Why, the dirty, double-crossin' polecats, pullin' such a trick. Here, set down. I'll have some breakfast on the table pronto. Won't take no time. There's plenty left an' still warm."

A considerable crowd had gathered for the funeral. Some men had liked Tom Harkness, others had hated him, but all had respected him for a forthrightly honest man according to his code. Most of them, friends and enemies alike, were sorry to see him go. As one of the latter remarked, chewing and spitting philosophically toward the edge of the open grave:

"When you don't have somebody like him to cuss, it kind of leaves you with only yoreself to blame for yore troubles—and that ain't no pleasure."

Vick was taking charge of the funeral ceremonies, more or less as a matter of course. No preacher was available to conduct the last rites, and so, as he remarked, it seemed to sort of devolve on him, as an old friend and partner of the deceased, to make a few remarks.

Today, Vick's voice had taken on a new quality. It was no longer irritable and domineering. In a black suit donned for the occasion, he might, outwardly at least, have been almost a sky pilot himself.

"Words are sort of a waste at a time like this," he began, looking around on the crowd. "Everybody knows any of the good things that might be said about a man like Tom Harkness, to start with. But it sure wouldn't be fitting if we didn't say them."

He paused for effect, went on.

"This ain't an old country, as places go. But one of the first settlers in these parts was Tom. He and the country, they sort of grew together. And I mean that. There's always some men that build a country up, just like there's others that try to tear it down. Tom Harkness was one of those who built.

"But when you do things in a big way, you always make some people mad. They can't stand to see anybody else succeed. So they've got to start tearin' down. And the easiest way to do that is to get the fellow that's getting somewhere. That's what the Lone Pine—or mebby I ought to say the fellow that's come in to this country and is tryin' to make out he's Lone Pine—that's what he did to Harkness!"

A murmur of approval, which was half a growl, went up. Vick's voice rose a little.

"Some people give flowers for the dead, an' let it go at that. I reckon we can give something better than that, in this case—somethin' that means a lot more. Such as cleanin' a country up, and wipin' out a nest of skunks. When it comes to murder and the kidnappin' of women, that's going a lot too far for any country. You all know what I mean."

His eulogy of Harkness had turned into a diatribe against Calhoun and Lone Pine, but it was accomplishing the purpose that he desired. When he finished, Vick was well satisfied with the results. Things were going his way at last. It lacked only one piece of news to make it a perfect day, and that news came with startling promptness. As he stepped back from the funeral oration, someone plucked at his sleeve. It was Bender, the cookee from Window Sash, his face curiously excited.

"I got 'em for you, over here," he said.

"What do you mean?" Vick demanded, and lowered his voice nervously. "What you talkin' about?"

"Calhoun—an' the girl." Bender jerked a thumb toward a big wagon, standing near the outskirts of the crowd, and there was a cruel elation in his face

191

which was like the dankness of wind after rain.
"They're in that. They come to the house to get
some breakfast. Trant, he'd tried to stop 'em at the
river, but Calhoun took his gun away from him. I
gave 'em some breakfast—and put some dope in
their coffee. They're under that tarp, sleepin' like
logs."

Vick's breath quickened with excitement. It had
cost a good deal to maintain one or more spies on
every surrounding ranch, but now that investment
was beginning to pay dividends. The cookee at
Window Sash had been one of the least important-
seeming of them all, but looks could be deceiving.
There was a quality in this man which Vick had
never sensed before.

"What you want done with 'em?" Bender asked.
The shadow of a grin creased his leathery face and
exposed a brown snaggle tooth. "I heard some of
what you was sayin' to the crowd. Reckon they're
in a mood to string Calhoun up, if yuh say the
word."

"No, no," Vick said hastily, and some of the
brightness of the day seemed to fade. It struck him
that some of his own words about cleaning a country up could be prophetic unless things were
handled just right.

"No one must know that they're here. The two

of them unconscious, and together—that would spoil everything. Nobody would think of lynching him till he was conscious, and they'd hear the girl talk." He wet his lips nervously.

"You've got to get them away from here—pronto. To some place where they'll be safe for a while—where nobody will come fooling around—"

"I know just the place," Bender agreed. "That old homestead shack of Harkness, on the edge of the prairie."

"That'll do," Vick agreed. "Get them there. I'll be along, soon as I can make it, to talk to them."

Calhoun stirred and tried to sit up, and found it hard to move at all. Something was wrong. His head ached, his mouth felt furry, something interfered with his arms and legs. He rolled a little, and was wider awake, suddenly tense and nervous.

Something was radically wrong. And then he made the discovery that his hands were tied behind his back, his ankles fastened together as well. He was lying on a bare, dusty floor, in a room completely empty of any furniture, and with a musty, stuffy odor. The ancient paper on the walls was faded and cracked and stained.

That was surprising enough. The difficult thing was to remember, for his head was confused. The

193

last he could recall—now he had it—he and Shirley had reached Window Sash and eaten breakfast. That, and drinking a cup of coffee, was the last thing he could recollect.

A small, fugitive ray of sunshine crept in at a point by the window and touched the floor at his feet. It came from a crack in the boarded up window, he saw. That much he could tell, as he struggled to sit up, and, after considerable effort, managed to do so, legs outstretched before him. His head was clearing fast now, and his mind was bitter.

It was clear enough what had happened. That cookee had drugged their coffee, had been able to do so because there, at Shirley's home, was the last place they had expected to run into trouble. Now he was here—wherever that was. Where was Shirley, and what was next on the program?

The probable answers were not pleasant ones. That sunshine looked to him as though it must come from an angle which would indicate that it was afternoon. That was logical enough, for it would take hours for the effects of the drug to wear off. That would mean that Tom Harkness had been buried for hours, and that the *coup* which he and Shirley had planned to pull off so devastatingly had failed completely.

Struggling at his bonds, he grunted. He couldn't

194

really blame himself for what had happened. It was one of those things impossible to foresee or guard against, for the thing had happened at Window Sash. But there was only a cold comfort in that. His bonds were tight—so tight that his arms were almost numb, his legs seemed to be asleep. Too tight to get them loose.

He tensed a little, and then it came again—the sound of voices, growing louder. There was the tramp of boots on bare, echoing floors. One of the voices he recognized readily enough as the domineering basso of Vick. The other one, after a little, he identified as that of the treacherous cookee.

"I got them in two diff'rent rooms, just to be sure," Bender was explaining. "Though there ain't been nobody around here, nothin' to bother."

"It's a good place, all right," Vick agreed. "And you did good work this morning. I won't forget about it."

The door opened, and the two of them came in. They stopped at the sight of Calhoun, awake and sitting up. Vick's gaze took him in, and an unpleasant smile curved the mouth of the boss of Wagon Wheel.

"So you're awake, eh?" he asked. "How do you like it?"

"I can think of things that would suit me better," Calhoun returned dryly.

"Such as danglin' in a rope?" Vick taunted. "Mebby you'll be doing just that, pretty soon. You was the hombre that figgered to come in here and push me around, I seem to recollect. I had you brought here because I wanted a talk with you before that hangin'—but things have got to the point now where you ain't important any more."

He shrugged, and gestured to Bender, who fitted a key into the lock of another door on the opposite side of the room, and they passed through and closed it again. But sounds came clearly enough for Calhoun to tell that Shirley was in the next room, and likewise awake now.

"You didn't have to tie her so tight," Vick said harshly. "Don't you have any sense?"

"She ain't tied near as tight as he is," Bender protested. "But I didn't want to take any chances."

"I'm right sorry about this, Shirley," Vick said, "I didn't aim—"

"Save your breath," Shirley said scornfully. "I'd rather listen to a cow bawling."

"What do you mean by that?" Vick demanded.

"They only bawl when they mean it. And they don't lie every time they open their mouths."

"I don't know what you're gettin' at—"

"Don't pretend. And don't think you can fool

me. My dad was murdered because of your orders —and then you pretend to be a friend of his. I know all about you."

"You've got me all wrong, Shirley," Vick protested. "Your dad was a friend of mine. I guess maybe Doyle killed him, but I sure didn't know a thing about it, or want it to happen that way."

"Did you tell the people, this morning, that it was Doyle who did it?" Shirley demanded. Then, as he was silent, she laughed scornfully again.

"You're just as much a killer as Doyle. And just as much responsible."

Vick hesitated, taken aback, rage and fear growing in him.

"You ain't helpin' things any, talkin' that way to me," he warned. "I come here, aimin' to help you out. I was thinkin' if you'd marry me, I could take care of you—"

"Marry you?" Shirley repeated, amazed, then laughed again.

"So you thought of that, just as soon as I inherited Window Sash," she taunted. "A nice idea— taking care of me!"

"Be a lot better for you as my wife than not," Vick warned, his anger getting the better of him.

"And for you, since a wife can't testify against her husband, if he happens to be a murderer!" Shirley flashed. "I'd rather die a thousand times!"

"Either you'll keep a civil tongue in yore head, girl, or mebby you will die!" Vick growled.

Shirley was undaunted by the threat.

"Where do you think you'd get, murdering me?" she asked. "It would be found out. You can't cover up everything."

Vick and his henchman exchanged glances.

"I was hopin' you'd be reasonable," Vick said. "And I sure gave you a chance. But since you won't —well, I ain't so big a fool as to leave you the chance to do any talkin'—not when things are coming along so nice as they are."

He turned and tramped back into the other room. Shirley blanched a little at that, and some of the defiance ebbed out of her. Somehow, up to then, she hadn't believed that he would go so far as murder—not in her case, at least. But she saw now that she had underestimated the man. Having embarked upon a course, he would stop at nothing to achieve his purpose. The door closed again, and Vick spoke harshly to Calhoun.

"I'd aimed to have a talk with you—but it won't be necessary now. If them ropes are troublin' you, enjoy how tight they feel. You won't be able to feel much longer!"

198

17

The two turned and tramped on out, slamming the door behind them. Vick was tugging at the lobe of his left ear thoughtfully as the pair reached the outer air.

"We got to get rid of both of 'em," he growled, staring at the side of the hill against which one edge of the house was backed up. "I kind of wanted to save the girl—but she'd see me hang for my pains, if I did."

"We can't afford to take no chances with either of 'em," Bender agreed readily.

"That's right. What I'm wonderin' about is the best way to do it. Don't want no traces of them to turn up. I'd like to have Calhoun hung, but he might get a chance to talk. Can't risk that. Be better if the two of them just disappeared. Folks think now that he's kidnapped her, or that they've eloped. They'll figure he got out of the country, when he knew he was licked anyway—"

"Or if they don't think that, they can't prove anything, anyway," Bender agreed. "That's all that matters."

"Yeah. You got any ideas—"

Vick stopped. A horseman was riding up the coulee, his horse lathered and blowing. His voice cracked a little at sight of his employer.

"You got to come a-runnin'," he panted. "Seems like hell's broke loose. Unless you can get it under control, right pronto—"

Vick listened, and his face whitened a little under its tan. He thought again that perhaps his words of the morning had been unconsciously, even ironically prophetic. He turned toward where his horse cropped the short grass, then swung back indecisively.

"We got to get rid of that pair first," he jerked out. "And we can't leave any bodies to be found—"

"Why not touch a match to them weeds at the

corners of the house?" Bender suggested, and his voice had an avid cruelty which was like the flicking tongue of a serpent. "It's a big place—and dry. Nobody'll come till it's ashes. There won't be nothin' to be found by then."

For a moment, revulsion shone in Vick's face, and he looked at the cookee as though beholding a strange and unlovely sort of a worm. Up to a few days ago, Vick had held two ambitions, each of about equal importance. He had been determined to win land and power for himself, to be the big man in this whole section of country.

Along with that, he had wished to appear as a big man in other ways—as a sort of glorified country squire, liked and respected by his neighbors, as became a man of the position he intended to fill.

The two ambitions had not often clashed. Rather, they had seemed until recently to belong together, to go hand in hand. But of late they had been in increasingly sharp conflict. Now to attain the one it was more and more necessary to trample ruthlessly on the other. He had done so already often enough, so that it was not too hard to do now.

"Mebby you're right," he agreed slowly. "I don't just like it—"

"It'll do a clean job," Bender argued. "I'll stick around to see that nothing goes wrong."

"All right," Vick gave in. "See that you do—for it's your neck as well as mine, now." He turned, and spurred, and swiped at his face with his sleeve as he rode. He was sweating, but it was a cold and clammy sweat. When, near the mouth of the long coulee, he turned to glance back, he saw smoke already mounting in a column, and flames beginning to race hungrily along the tinder-dry sides of the old shack.

Doyle was like a man in torment. He could no longer think clearly, because of the mounting pain and fever. It was more the instinct of a sick animal than anything else which drove him back to the creek, and he lay there and plunged his burning arm deep in the cold water, drinking deeply. He even slept a little.

When he roused, he felt better. The pain and fever, by some freakish trick, had abated somewhat, enough so that he could think again. Coupled with that was an urgent sense of hunger. He could not remember when he had last eaten, but it was a long time ago. It came to him that he needed food to keep going.

The logical place to get it was Lone Pine. It was not far to the house, and he could slip in and get something to eat. More, he ought to be able to get a horse there. Beyond that, he did not plan.

Everything seemed quiet when he came in sight of the buildings. He could still smell the ashes from the burnt bunk house, and his upper lip lifted in a snarl, like that of a savage dog, at the memory. That scheme had seemed to promise so well, but all his trouble had really stemmed from it.

He was nearing the house when he heard a door open softly, and shrank back into the deeper gloom. Again, for a while, he was alert, a creature of the night, perfectly at home in the dark. But what he saw jarred him rudely, and made him wonder for a moment just how sick he was, if his imagination was playing tricks on him.

But it was real enough. The man who walked there, as erect and able as anyone else, was Sam Troupe. Gone was all semblance of the cripple he had long pretended to be. He was heading for the barn now, and Doyle, forgetting his hunger in wonder at this new development, followed where he could keep an eye on him.

Troupe entered the barn, moving in the deeper gloom with a sureness which testified that this was not his first visit to it. He bridled a horse in one of the stalls, led it out, and threw on a saddle with easy expertness. Then he led it outside and left it stand, while he moved back to the house after something, going with all the stealth of a stalking cat.

Doyle made good use of the delay to saddle another horse for himself. There were three in the barn, and he took the handiest one, congratulating himself that it appeared to be gentle and willing. It stood while he heaved the saddle on, which helped, for working one-handed was not easy. But now excitement lent him strength.

Presently, when Troupe came out again and swung into the saddle and rode away, Doyle followed him. Understanding was beginning to come come to him now. He had long known that Sam Troupe was contankerous and unpleasant, making a general nuisance of himself, and he had suspected that Marjorie had little liking for the man.

But it had never occurred to him, nor, apparently, to anyone else, that Troupe was deliberately playing a part; that in reality he was not crippled at all. Yet that was clear enough now, and Doyle remembered that the man had been bitter at his half-brother, Marjorie's father, claiming that he was a rich man while he had nothing. Yet before his injury, Sam Troupe had always been known as a lazy wastrel.

Doyle was interested in seeing what he was up

to. There had long been mysteries connected with Lone Pine, and it looked as if this was one of the biggest.

He was puzzled, presently, to see Troupe swing off to a little hidden pasture, deep in a canyon, and come out of it with a lone steer which he drove ahead of him. It was a big roan, and seemed to be well trained.

After about a mile, they came to the two-year-olds which Calhoun had brought back across Cayuse. They were bedded down for the night, but Troupe roused them up and got them moving with all the skill of an old hand. And now the big roan steer was taking the lead, doing it as though this were all an old story. With a leader, the others followed readily.

Doyle's excitement was mounting. What was Troupe up to? He had a strong suspicion, but he wanted to see it with his own eyes before he would believe it.

The herd was heading, not at the usual slow pace which a man took to drive cattle, but almost at a trot, for the creek, well below the regular crossing. Finally they sighted the Cayuse, the waters a broad, dark sheen here, for at this point it spread out and ran lazily. The place appeared to be a perfect crossing. More than one man had learned, to his regret, how deceptive the Cayuse could be here. This was the worst stretch of quicksand anywhere on the creek.

But Doyle already had a pretty good idea what was going to happen, and he was not much surprised when the big roan steer, without hesitation, walked straight out into the water. The others, used now to his leadership, and with Troupe urging them along behind, followed.

By rights, they should already have been in trouble, sinking deep in the clutching sands, bawling and struggling against the sucking death from the depths. But nothing of the sort was happening. The roan steer was going ahead, picking its way with an uncanny sureness; the others were strung out behind. And they were crossing the Cayuse safely.

It was all clear enough to Doyle now. The roan was a bellwether, a Judas, trained to lead others. Doyle had seen such an animal once, in the stockyards of a big city; a sleek, fat steer that led others unsuspectingly straight to the slaughter, repeating the thing over and over again. This big roan, equally well trained and apparently enjoying his job just as much, was doing the same thing right here.

There was one difference. Here was none of the

blood and stench of slaughter pens, and once safely across the Cayuse, the roan had no way of knowing that he had guided a herd to destruction. But it was no surprise to Doyle to see other horsemen waiting on the far bank. This explained a lot that had been happening on Lone Pine of late years.

Marjorie Johnson was hard-working, and supposed to be a pretty good manager. Her father before her had been the same. But both had been up against something they did not even guess at. Here was the mystery of the disappearing herds which depleted Lone Pine and turned it from a profitable spread into a liability.

The last of the herd were out in the water now, and Sam Troupe, pausing only long enough to cut a willow stick and stick it out at the edge of the creek, was following them. He rode with easy sureness in the path which they had followed.

Coming closer, Doyle could see that the willow stick was lined with a boulder on the far bank, and with another on this side. Near it, but at one side, was another and similar-appearing boulder. Doyle eyed it all with lively interest, his arm almost forgotten.

Somehow, Sam Troupe had learned of this safe passageway here, where none was supposed to exist. Jealous and scheming, hiding behind the cloak of a cripple, he had worked to make money for himself, not caring if he ruined Lone Pine in the process.

As Doyle had heard the story, the man had been thrown from a horse years before, his spine injured, leaving him crippled. Perhaps he hadn't been able to walk for a while. Later, when he had regained the use of his legs, he had carefully kept that fact hidden.

And at night he had rustled from Lone Pine, stealing from his half-brother and later from his niece. A few at a time, taken down here, could disappear without leaving a trace. On the far shore, they landed where no one would ever suspect that cattle could come, and were driven away by confederates in perfect safety. No one would look for them on that side of Cayuse.

Probably Troupe had figured on ruining Lone Pine and eventually getting it for himself. Vick's plans had interfered, so tonight, with time apparently growing short for the ranch, Troupe was stealing on a bigger, wholesale scale.

Now he was across the creek and out of sight, along with those who had been waiting there. Getting paid, probably. Then he would figure to be back and safely in his room again before anyone stirred around the ranch house. If anyone looked in, they would probably see a dummy in the bed, and assume that he was sleeping. Because of his irascible nature, no one would be apt to disturb him until it was necessary, in the morning.

Doyle chuckled to himself. This had taken his mind off himself and his own troubles. In addition, it offered him a good way out. He'd cross here, a little later, and be in town by morning.

But before that, he'd play a little trick on the trickster himself. He had never liked Troupe, and it would be doing a kindness to Marjorie to rid her of the incubus. There were times, rare enough, when he took pleasure in doing someone else a good turn.

He was about to move out of the brush when he saw something coming. It was the roan steer. It crossed back safely and disappeared in the brush. Probably Troupe had some other confederate to help him, at times, with this steer. But since he probably counted this as the last raid that he would ever make on the herds, he wasn't paying too much attention to it now.

Doyle pulled up the freshly cut willow and moved it a little. Now it was still in line with a boulder, but not the same big stone. From even halfway across the stream, in light like this, a man could not see that it was the wrong boulder.

That done, Doyle drew back again, out of sight, chuckling. He had not long to wait. Presently Troupe, riding easily, came out of the brush on the opposite shore; his horse waded out and started back across. And now, without the sure instinct of the roan steer to guide him, Troupe was taking no chances. He was watching that willow and the line of the boulder beyond, setting his course by it. Probably he had done it many times before.

He was halfway across before the change made any difference. Then, abruptly, his horse was floundering, making desperate efforts to free itself from suddenly clutching sands. In its panic, it swung the wrong way, and its rider, taken equally by surprise, could not turn it back in time.

And now Doyle was given a demonstration of the swiftness of the power in those sands. The horse could not pull free, try as it would. It was going down fast. Its rider, terrified, sprang off and tried to fight his way back to the safe zone, and failed. He took three or four steps, and could go no farther. Doyle watched him, and he had only one regret. Troupe was going down, probably, with a pocketful of money. But money was of no use in such a situation.

His head was still above water when Doyle rode out and casually changed the willow again, for his own guidance. Seeing him, the doomed man screamed for help. His scream was still ringing when he choked, and then a sort of false peace settled over the gently rippling sands.

18

Calhoun sat quietly for a minute, after the receding footsteps of the two men had died away. Then, convinced that they were really out of hearing and not coming back, he wasted no time. The threat in Vick's last words had been too implicit to ignore.

Already, he was hitching his way along the floor toward that door which opened into the next room where Shirley was a captive. He raised his voice.

"Let's see if we can get this door open, Shirley."

"Right with you—as soon as I—can roll," Shirley's voice came back, and if there was any undercurrent of dismay, it was well hidden.

Calhoun reached the door, hitching around until his back was against it. It was a strain to raise his bound hands so that he could get hold of the knob, but he managed it. He twisted, and fresh dismay coursed like an icy shock through him. He had known that the door had been locked when they first came, but he hadn't seen them lock it again.

Yet it had been done, as an added measure of precaution. Calhoun edged away from it.

"Keep away from the door, Shirley," he called. "I'm going to try kicking it down."

That job might be like trying to move a balky cayuse. The thing would be comparatively easy, if he could get at it or exert his strength. But tied as he was, it was hard to move at all, and his cramped, aching legs seemed to have no power left in them. Yet he had to move fast now, or they would be too late even to make a fight against whatever Calhoun and Bender had in mind for them.

Hunched up, lying on his back a little way from the door, Calhoun drew both feet up together and lashed at the barricade. They hit it, but served only to jar it. It would take a lot more than that, he saw, to be effective.

Moving a little closer, he tried again. Three times,

and then something gave. One hinge was off. Again he kicked, then rolled up against the swaying remnants and crawled through into the next room.

Like his own, it was bare enough, save for Shirley. She was tied in much the same fashion as himself; her face was smudged with dust, white with strain and fatigue. But she managed to smile at him as he came crawling and rolling through.

"You look like one of these armadillos, or something, coming through there," she said. "Or one of these long-behinds that has to travel around the side of a hill. Even at that, you're a sight for sore eyes."

"The last part of that goes double," Calhoun grunted, and forced a grin. "I never knew before just how handy big feet could be. Sure have their uses, though. And now, if you'll excuse me turnin' my back on you—"

It was a strained attempt at lightness, but it helped. Back to back, sitting there on the floor, they could at least work rather fumblingly at each other's bonds. But working in such a cramped position, with fingers already half numb, it was agonizingly slow work against tight knots.

"Better let me try," Calhoun suggested. "Likely you're not tied quite as tight as I am."

He worked doggedly, forced to do everything

by feeling, which was uncertain at best.

"Do you know where we are?" he asked.

"Yes," Shirley agreed. "This is the house that I was born in."

Calhoun was startled. He hadn't figured on them being taken so far from Window Sash, but it was, after all, a logical move. This was one place where no one would ever look for them, where people rarely came. What happened here would go unnoticed, at least until it was all over with.

"We must have been under those knockout powders a lot longer than I figured," he said finally.

"I guess so," Shirley agreed. "I'm sorry. It—it sort of seems as if it was my fault, happening there at our ranch, and all."

"It wasn't your fault at all," he denied almost harshly. "How could you figure he'd double-cross us? Anyway, I think this knot's startin' to loosen a little."

"I think so, too," Shirley agreed. "Do you hear something?"

Calhoun had been hearing it now for the last two or three minutes. At first he had been undecided, but the noise was becoming too steady and loud to be mistaken any longer. He was working feverishly, but trying to hold himself steady, to avert any wasted effort.

"Yeah, I hear it," he said dryly.

"It—it sounds as though they'd set fire to the house," Shirley whispered.

"Sounds that way," Calhoun admitted matter of factly. "But it'll be a while before it really gets going."

He wasn't sure whether she would believe that or not. He didn't believe it himself. Unless his ears were playing him tricks, fire had been started at all four corners of the house. Now a faint smell of smoke came to their nostrils, and the sound of the racing flames was louder. He worked feverishly. Unless they got loose and out pretty soon, it would be too late to get out at all.

"I didn't think anyone would do such a beastly thing!" Shirley whispered tensely.

"When it comes to saving their own necks, some folks will do anything," Calhoun said. "Now I'm getting that knot. Just a second. Now see if you can pull a hand loose."

"Yes. It's loose." Shirley's voice quivered with excitement. "Now let me get at you."

She turned, a little clumsily, but at least she could see what she was doing, and she had the use of her hands. But Calhoun knew that her fingers were stiff and fumbling, and she was working with frantic desperation.

"Take it easy," he encouraged. "We'll have time to figure something out now. They didn't count on us getting loose at all."

She steadied a little at the calmness of his voice, but Calhoun was wracking his brains, trying to figure a way out. Shirley spoke, voicing his thoughts.

"Even when we get loose, how can we get out?" she asked. "They'll probably wait around and keep watch until they're sure that it's all burnt and us with it. If we try to run out, we'll be shot as soon as we get outside. They can't afford anything else, now."

That was the worst rub—though not the only one. The window in this room, as in the other one, was boarded up from the outside. It would be a slow, hard job to knock off boards enough to get out. And the doors would probably be in the same shape as the windows—enveloped in flames before they could get through them.

For the fire was gaining rapid headway, and there was no longer any doubt that it had been started on all four sides. The sound of the flames was growing to a steady, ominous crackle; the reflection of them shone in through the window like a beacon of doom. Smoke was beginning to eddy into the room from several points.

The tinder-dry boards were burning like pitch,

and it would be only a matter of minutes until the whole structure would be a torch. Sudden scarlet raced across the outside of the window, red tongues began to lick through the cracks of the boards and then, inside, to lengthen and reach hungrily toward the ceiling, catching on the old, torn wall paper.

Already it was too late to get out there. Probably it would be too late to get out anywhere, even if there was no gunman standing a death-watch outside. By the time his hands were free, and they could untie their feet, it would be hopeless.

But Shirley's voice now was steady, confident.

"I've just remembered something!" she said. "Something that they won't know about. Maybe we'll fool them yet. Now I've got that knot!"

She gave a jerk, and Calhoun felt the cords loosen about his wrists. It was agony to bring his arms around in front of him again, to start work without loss of time on the rope which tied his ankles together. He would have preferred to take it more gradually, while the circulation was restored in his arms and fingers, but Shirley had lost no time in going to work on him. Even now, she was bending forward to try to free her own feet.

The heat from the flames at the window was making itself felt now, and then, through the twisted, broken door, still hanging drunkenly by the upper hinge, smoke commenced to billow in, and there was more fire rolling along behind it. There were only the two exits from the room, and both were infernos of flame. But Shirley still seemed confident.

Whoever had tied his feet had done a good job. He had used, not a rope, but a length of rawhide, and it was drawn so tight that it was impossible even to get at the knots. Calhoun hitched across the floor to where a splinter from the broken door lay. He held it to the fire, the mounting heat almost searing his face, then backed away a little as his torch began to burn and applied the fire to the stretched rawhide between his ankles. After a moment it popped loose.

Shirley had had better luck. She had not been tied quite so tightly to begin with, else he could never have freed her wrists. Now she was getting unsteadily to her feet, and Calhoun tried to emulate her example. He stood up, but his feet were wooden. He swayed then, despite himself, and would have fallen had not Shirley caught him, bracing herself against him.

They stood swaying for a moment, in each other's arms, locked like the props of a stake and rider fence. Then Shirley dropped on hands and knees, and he saw that she was tugging at something. It was a trap door—so cleverly fitted in the floor that it had escaped his observation before, and apparently unused for years. It was stuck fast.

There was an iron ring. He got hold of it and tugged, and the door came open, revealing a yawning pit of blackness down below, an old, rickety-looking stairs leading down from the door.

Shirley seemed confident, however, and sure of herself. She descended rapidly, and Calhoun followed. The flare of light up above, showing through the open trap door, gave a little light down below, but not much. If this was just a cellar, it would only postpone their fate. Once the house was well afire above them, and then collapsed in a heap—

Down here, however, the air was still cool, free from smoke, and they could again draw a deep breath. Calhoun tried to look around. There were apparently no windows leading out of here, no outer door.

"Isn't there any way out of here?" he asked.

"No regular way," Shirley said. "But there's something else. I hope it's still all right."

She led him over to one side, over to the hill against which the house sat. For a few moments, Calhoun could see nothing. Then he made out what looked like a hole in the side of the wall, leading back.

Shirley's voice was almost gay.

"It seems to be as good as ever," she said. "My private cave! If we're back in there, I don't think the fire will bother us much. And it can't reach us, even if the house does fall down over us."

"I guess not," Calhoun agreed, still puzzled. "But what is it?"

"My cave," Shirley explained. "When I was just a little girl, and we lived here, I had a great imagination. And I liked to dig. I'd heard somewhere about how pioneers used to dig secret passageways from their house back into a hill, so as to have a hiding place in case of Indian attack, and I thought it was a fine idea. There was an outer entrance to this room then, and plenty of light and air. That was closed up, later on.

"So I spent hours down here, for weeks, digging this. Of course, most of the work was done by two or three cowboys, and I used to rope them in and boss the job. I even got Dad—" Her voice caught for a moment. "He helped me some, too, though he disapproved of the whole thing."

Her voice came back to him, muffled, for she was crawling back inside now. Calhoun followed, on hands and knees. It was none too big for him, but he saw that, back in a few feet, it had been widened out into a small room.

"Be careful," she said. "I've still got a few of my old dolls and trinkets in here. Dad put some props in so it wouldn't cave down on me. When I dug it, I—I made myself believe that some day my life might depend on it."

"Looks like you had a sort of second sight," Calhoun said huskily. Now, even from back in here, they could hear the increasing roar of the fire, the sharp crack of falling timbers, and the reflection of the firelight was increasing. Soon the cellar would be full of flaming debris. Methodically, he set about to make a barricade in the entrance-tunnel, to stop the searing heat and gas which would come with the flames.

19

Doyle reached town in the dawn, clinging doggedly to one purpose in his mind—to find the
medico. He had fought to keep that resolve fixed
in mind for the last couple of hours, repeating it
over and over, like a small boy learning a lesson;
clinging to it as he had clung to the saddle horn
with his good hand, to keep himself from tumbling.

Fortunately, his cayuse had headed for town
with little guidance. It seemed to realize that it
had a desperately sick man on its back, one who
was no longer capable of thinking or doing much

for himself. It had crossed Cayuse Creek gingerly, following the route taken by the cattle, and without mishap.

Doyle had been aware of that. Even then, though, the pain was commencing to flow back in a dizzy wave which surged through his arm and shoulder and spread through his whole body, and with it the fever was mounting again. It was as though, having receded for a little while, the return tide was higher than ever.

Caught in the relentless tide of it, he had not been particularly interested even in that crossing of the creek. If something went wrong and the sucking sands pulled him down, that was no longer such a dreadful thing to contemplate. Those waters looked very cool.

"Lucky devil," he muttered, remembering Troupe, and how the waters had closed so smoothly over him. "Nothin' to worry about down there."

But he had forgotten Troupe almost at once, and nearly everything else. His head, when it was not numb, was beclouded now with whirling fantasies which kept just beyond the borderline of reality, so that he was hard put to it to know what was real and what was fancy. One thing only he held fast to: that he must reach Doc Fenton.

A few early riders were at their tasks as he

came into town. Swampers sweeping out saloons, washing down windows. One man, who had lain drunk all night, was trying to pick himself up again, and not doing too well at it.

All of them eyed the lone horseman with a desultory sort of interest, which quickened as they recognized him, then became lively as they saw that his whole arm and side was bloody. Some of it was dry, dark blood, but some was fresh and red. And the man looked bad.

But no one cared to meddle with the gunman, even to help him, especially in that condition. Doyle's moods were notoriously erratic. And he seemed to know what he was doing. He was left alone as he rode to Doc Fenton's office, where his horse stopped of its own accord. Doc usually slept on a cot in a back room.

For a dragging minute, Doyle sat there, not aware that his horse had stopped, and even after he understood, he was puzzled as to what to do. He looked up and saw the sign, but it made no sense to his glazed eyes. It was the mumbling in his throat, an instinctive prodding, that made him dismount.

His horse stood still, patiently, and when he lost his hold and fell it did not shy away. Doyle lay there, nor was he aware of the scream which had issued from his throat as he struck on his broken arm. He was only half conscious when Doc, aroused by the noise, found him.

The funeral was over before Doc Fenton, his face set in stern lines, came out of his office. He had worked over Doyle with considerably more zeal than he had done when the gunman had first presented himself for attention, even with the certain knowledge today that whatever he did was wasted effort.

Doyle's injuries, while bad, had still amounted to little enough, when he had first taken them. With his capacity for standing punishment, he would soon have been as fit as ever again, had he taken care of himself and given nature a chance to do its work.

But now Fenton was appalled at the condition of the man, and the punishment he must have taken, blundering around, jolting his arm, falling on it, and all the rest.

Infection was already at an advanced stage. Even if he were to cut the arm off at the shoulder, Doc knew at once that it would do no good. The poison had spread too far to be stopped. It was only a matter of hours now, and then, surprisingly enough, Doyle would die, not with his boots on, but in bed.

Despite the certainty of that, Fenton had worked

on him to make him more comfortable, to clean him up and do what he could. Part of it was his professional job, and this time, he felt more than a little pity for the man. He must have suffered terribly.

There was a second, and even more potent reason, which held Doc to his post until Doyle finally sank off into a half-sleep, half-coma, from which Fenton knew that he would probably not awaken. Doyle, in the grip of fever, had talked. Some of it was wild raving, but some had held the ring of truth, and Fenton had listened.

Now, leaving his office, and discovering that the crowd which had attended the funeral had already dispersed, Fenton got his own horse and rode out of town, heading for Lone Pine.

He knew of the deadline at the creek, of the guards posted there. But he was in no mood to be halted. While listening to the ravings of Doyle, he had finally come to a decision, and now he was impatient to carry out a long delayed ambition. When he reached the Cayuse and someone challenged him sharply, he answered with equal curtness.

"I'm heading for Lone Pine, yes. And don't try to say I can't."

The guard—there was a second man who watched

in silence—was one of Vick's men. Now he shifted truculently, hitching his gun belt around ostentatiously.

"Our orders are to stop anybody an' everybody," he said shortly. "Reckon that includes you."

"I'm a doctor," Fenton reminded him. "And a doctor goes anywhere, any time."

"Not this time."

Fenton leaned forward in the saddle, and showed not the impassive, rather friendly face that most men knew, but a fighting face.

"I'm going to Lone Pine—now," he said. "And I'm coming back across here when I get good and ready. Try and shoot me, and you'll get strung up. I'm the only medico in this neck of the woods, and from the looks, there'll be plenty need of my services before too long!"

He turned, and pushed his horse out into the creek. The guard opened his mouth, looked at his silent, quizzical companion, and closed it again. There was much truth in what Doc had just said.

There was no trouble with the guard posted on the opposite side of Cayuse. Muskett was there, and he recognized Fenton, and was glad to see him. Doc, he knew, was a good friend of Miss Marjorie. And Doc was to be trusted.

"You can go right along up to the house if you feel that way, Doc," he said. "They'll be glad to see you, too, same as I am."

"Who will?" Fenton asked bluntly. "Who is there now? Anybody hurt?"

Muskett shook his head, and Fenton lost a little of his strained look.

"Not hurt, I guess. But near as bad. There's Miss Marjorie, an' Mrs. Henry. And they're worryin' their heads off, I guess. You see, Calhoun and Shirley Harkness started out last night to get across the creek—but seems like if they'd made it and told their story in town, things'd be diff'rent by now. Do you know whether they made it or not?"

"I don't think they've been seen at all," Fenton said. "If they have, I haven't heard of it."

They exchanged glances, both considering what that might mean.

"Sam Troupe's disappeared, too," Muskett went on. "And two of the horses. Can't find hide or hair of either of 'em. Me, I wouldn't cry none about him," he added grimly. "But it's mighty queer."

"Sounds so," Fenton agreed noncommittally, and rode on. He had never been called to look after Marjorie's uncle, though he and Marjorie were very good friends. He had sometimes thought it

229

a little queer that a cripple should not want at least to be checked over. Now he knew that he hadn't understood half the queerness. Muskett's story was proof that some of Doyle's ravings had not been so very wild.

The two women were at the house, and Marjorie's face lighted at sight of Fenton. Glades and DeMers were there as well. They asked eagerly for news.

"As for Calhoun and Shirley Harkness, I don't know a thing about them," Fenton confessed. "Apparently nobody has seen anything of them."

Everyone considered that in silence for a minute. It might mean one of two things. Either the treacherous Cayuse had another dark secret which it was not likely to tell, or they had been captured by some of those on guard. But that, considering Shirley's presence, seemed unlikely.

Marjorie, Fenton noted, was showing the strain of the last several days. She looked white and tired.

"There's another funny thing," she said. "Uncle Sam has disappeared. Just vanished, completely. Though how he could have—"

"Muskett told me about it," Fenton nodded. "Have you noticed anything about your two-year-olds that were brought home?"

Marjorie looked at him, puzzled by his words,

by the seemingly abrupt, almost callous change of subject.

"Why—why, no," she confessed. "We've been too busy and upset, I guess, to think much about them."

Fenton resolved to tell the bald truth. Sometimes it was easier to take.

"Doyle came into town early this morning," he said. "Fell off his horse in front of my door. He's in bad shape—infection in his arm. But he was able to talk some. Babbling with fever, but some of it seems to make sense. He was telling about seeing Sam Troupe—seeing him riding a horse last night, and driving those cattle across Cayuse at Quicksand Crossing—getting them across with a big roan Judas steer to lead them, and not being touched by the sands."

The others were staring at him, bewildered. Doc went on, inexorably.

"That seems to have been true, and to explain where your herds have been disappearing to for so long. He got them across, then sold them to some riders who were waiting on the other side—then he got caught in the quicksand himself, as he was coming back across."

"I always thought he was fakin', pretendin' that he couldn't walk," Glades growled.

There was shock in Marjorie's face, but no disbelief. Troupe had fooled them, but in little ways, here and there, his act had been wearing thin for a long time. Now, putting those pieces together, they found it easy to understand.

"I didn't think, mean as he was, that he'd do that to me," Marjorie half sobbed.

The others had quietly withdrawn. Doc Fenton, aside from his professional status, had always been a shy man. But now he found the courage to do what he had long dreamed about.

"You need a man to look after you, Marjorie," he said. "And I reckon I'm that man."

"I was wondering when you were going to get around to saying so," Marjorie murmured through her tears.

20

Fenton was a little appalled at the situation on Lone Pine. He had known pretty well how bad things were, but he discovered now that, deep down inside himself, he had been expecting big things from Calhoun; something more than most men could do, something akin to a sort of magic. It had seemed to him that the man who could stop Doyle as he had done could do almost anything.

He still clung to the hope that Calhoun would turn up again, somewhere, somehow. But that hope seemed to be a thin reed to cling to. The Cayuse was a notoriously treacherous stream, and no man knew that better than Fenton. To try crossing it by night was not calculated to be an exercise conducive to long life.

It was at that juncture that Sackett rode in, with news.

"I saw the boat they used drawn up on the far side, where they aimed to land," he announced. "That was about three-four hours ago. I worked to get some closer and have a better look, and was out of sight of it for mebby twenty minutes. When I got to where I could see again, it wasn't there."

"What d'you make of that?" DeMers asked, excited. "You think they came back and got it again?"

"What I think's that Vick, or his men, caught them when they landed, and forgot about the boat for a spell," Sackett said bluntly. "Fin'ly somebody remembered it, and they got it out of sight."

That sounded logical to Fenton, and it put a new light on things—and a new responsibility on his own shoulders.

"I'm going back across deadline," he announced, "and say a few things, and ask a few questions."

"I'm going with you," Marjorie said promptly. "I want to tell them a few things, too."

Fenton hesitated, considering the risk for her. Then he nodded. There was danger, but Marjorie was a woman to ride by her man's side, whatever came along.

Abel was in charge of the guards now, with some of his own and Vick's crew. He had been a little hesitant at first about some of the things to be done. But now, in charge here during Vick's absence, he had no qualms. Being boss gave him a pleasant sense of importance.

"Nobody can cross to this side," he called out, as Marjorie and Fenton started to cross. But the doctor did not even act as though he had heard. He kept on riding, Marjorie beside him. Abel scowled and yelled the warning a second time, and knew that they heard well enough. He half reached for his holstered gun, then thought better of it. You couldn't shoot at a woman, or at the medico. That was what they were depending on, of course.

"Be better, anyway, to have them over here and where we can watch 'em," he muttered, and waited.

Fenton, however, showed no disposition to wait calmly for things to happen. He was in a mood to make them happen, as his horse splashed through the shallows and up to where Abel waited.

"What have you fellows done with Calhoun— and Shirley Harkness?" he challenged sharply. And noted with satisfaction that now, in addition to members of the Wagon Wheel and Flying A crews, some men from town and other outfits had just ridden up to within hearing.

"What do you mean, what've we done with them?" Abel growled. "Reckon they've lit a shuck out of this country—though whether she's elopin' with him, or bein' kidnapped, is more'n I could say."

"I can," Marjorie interposed. "In fact, I've got a lot to say. And I'm going to say it all."

That was what Abel had been afraid of, once she was across and could not be turned back. But he merely groaned inwardly and wished for Vick. He saw no way to shut her up.

Marjorie told the story in stark detail—how Shirley had discovered her father, near this spot; and that he had been killed by someone from Wagon Wheel or Flying A. Abel opened his mouth to protest, but she gave him no chance.

She explained how Vick's crew had tried to stop Shirley, and how Shirley in turn had kept them from getting across. Here was something new for the outsiders to hear, and they were drinking it in. Their expression, as the recital continued, boded no good for Wagon Wheel—or even for himself as an associate of Vick, Abel reflected uneasily.

"The boat got across, all right, and was drawn

up on this side of the creek," Fenton added quietly. "That means just one thing—that some of you have captured them. If there's been any kidnapping, you and Vick are responsible, Abel."

Abel drew back nervously.

"First I knew of it," he protested. "If anything like that's happened, I ain't had no hand in it."

It was this news which the messenger had carried to Vick—that the truth was coming out at last, and the public, which that morning had been solidly behind them, was now turning actively hostile. The blockade of Lone Pine was already at an end.

Vick rode, his mind in a turmoil. It might still be possible to salvage something out of the wreckage. With Calhoun gone, and Shirley Harkness as well, the picture was different. Window Sash would now be land open for the taking, and if he could not have Lone Pine, Window Sash would do just as well.

There had been no leadership under Abel, of course, no bearing down at the moment of crisis. But Vick knew that he had gone so far now that there was no longer any point in hesitating, no matter how ruthless the course to be followed. And most opposition would dissolve if faced with ruthlessness. Most of them were like Abel, in a pinch.

Well, he knew what to do. But when he sighted a group of men who had been friends and neighbors that morning, his blood chilled a little. It would take some fast talking to convince them this time.

There were six of them, and he reflected bleakly that that was about the odds which he had imposed on Calhoun. He didn't like to think about Calhoun now. It still gave him a queasy feeling at the pit of his stomach. Ordinary killing didn't affect him that way. But this thing had been different. He glanced with sharp distaste toward Bender, who had overtaken him a few minutes before, with the comment that the job was done.

The six questioned him sharply concerning Calhoun and Shirley. Vick insisted with equal sharpness that he knew no more about them than what he had told that morning. He'd been hunting, hoping to find some trace of them, it was true. He spread his hands and shrugged his shoulders, and appealed to the Window Sash cookee for confirmation.

"Ain't that so, Bender?"

"Sure it's so," Bender agreed, and looked suddenly uneasy. Vick saw why. Three more riders were coming toward them. One was Doc Fenton. Two were other members of the Window Sash.

"We've been lookin' all over for you," Fenton greeted them curtly. "Where you been, Vick?"

Vick shrugged and repeated what he had said before. But his uneasiness was growing. If only some of his own crew would show up—but you could count on it that they'd never be around when wanted. It had a smell of trouble, and he didn't like it.

The pair from Window Sash were eying Bender in amazement.

"What you doing here?" they demanded. "Thought we left you to look after things at the ranch."

Fenton pricked up his ears. Bender was a new man in the country, but he remembered him now, and his job at Window Sash.

"Calhoun and Shirley crossed Cayuse in a boat last night," Doc said, looking at Vick but speaking to all of them. "They got across all right, too. We saw the boat, drawn up on this side. But they've disappeared."

"It's like I've been tellin' you all along," Vick insisted. "Either they've eloped, or he's kidnapped her—"

"Maybe Bender can tell us something about that,"

Fenton added softly. "For they'd planned to head for Window Sash, to get horses and go on to town."

Bender shook his head.

"Never saw ary sign of them there, up to close to noon, when I left," he pronounced.

The others from Window Sash exchanged glances, and Vick felt a fresh qualm of uneasiness.

"He's lying," one of them pronounced flatly. "Sam and me got back there the middle of the forenoon, and he wasn't there then. And a couple of people had been there and had breakfast after the rest of us pulled out for town. The dirty dishes was still on the table."

The bluster was all gone out of Vick by now, replaced by a feeling as though ice had formed on his stomach. That was evidence only too easy to add up, and this fool of a cookee had been riding with him—had even backed his own alibi. It seemed to Vick that he could already feel the rough hair of a rope around his own throat.

A snarl rose in it, directed at Bender. Vick had been about to ask if the cookee had been lying to him, too. But he choked it down. He was equally guilty with Bender in what had happened, and if he turned on the man now, he knew that Bender was ready to betray him in turn. That wouldn't do.

"Reckon there's been a mistake somewhere," he grunted. "Bender's been with me for quite a spell. We sure ain't had anything to do with whatever's been going on. But I aim to find out who *has*, and and get to the bottom of it."

It was a good speech, but not so well received as the one he had made that morning. However, it served to let him get away from them, and Vick intended to make the most of his chance. He turned to Bender as soon as they were out of sight.

"We're in a bad spot," he said. "We've got just one chance. Hunt up my crew. Then, if it comes to trouble, we'll give 'em all they want of it."

"Pretty dangerous, ain't it?" Bender asked dubiously. "I thought you had things under control, but you sure as blazes have lost it. If it comes to a fight, we've too many ag'in' us. Be better to get out while we can."

"That might do for you, but how about me?" Vick demanded impatiently. "I've got property in this country. I can't run off and leave it." He added meaningly. "I got something in mind to give them more fight than they'll have any stomach for, if it comes to that. Stick with me, and I'll make it worth your while."

"You'd better," Bender agreed cynically. "Property's no good to a dead man."

241

There was too much truth in that for Vick's taste. Savagery boiled in him. He had been so very sure of everything only that morning. What had happened to spoil it all? Somehow it still seemed incredible.

But he had meant exactly what he said to Bender; he had a plan in mind, and was in the mood for using it. It was a long way to Wagon Wheel headquarters, but there was a line cabin not far off. And it contained what he needed.

Vick headed for it, and saw with satisfaction that everything was as he had counted on. He and a couple of his men had been doing some blasting near there a few weeks back. A trickle of water had come from under a big pile of boulders, the only water within miles. It had been his theory that, if those stones were ripped apart and a fissure in the crack enlarged, there would be plenty of water for a lot of cattle, instead of only a promise.

That was one theory which he had proved correct, and he could see the spring now, flowing in a small stream for some distance before it was lost in the ground. There was still some dynamite left at the shack, with fuses and caps. And he knew how to use the stuff.

Vick worked efficiently, not hurrying, for half an hour. When he rode away again, he carried an innocent-looking little package which was in reality a highly efficient bomb. If thrown violently, it would detonate as it struck. And if it came to a pinch, that was something that would be powerfully argumentative. Far more so, at close quarters with a mob, than a pair of six-guns.

Now, if Bender had just found his crew and rounded them up, he'd take control again. That was the good thing about such men as Bender and Doyle. Such ruthlessness as he planned on would make ordinary men quail. But not them. And he was the man to lead such a crew.

He was laughing softly to himself as he rode, pushing those other, ghastly memories to the far fringe of his mind. A man was a fool to think of those things, and he was no fool—

Vick halted abruptly, jerking his horse almost back on its haunches, yet not conscious that he had done so. Shock coursed through him like flame running in dynamite fuse. He had just topped a rise, where he could see for a considerable distance.

There was the road, just beyond, leading out from Sage, off toward Cayuse Creek and Lone Pine beyond. There was the shortcut ahead, which men sometimes used when they were in a hurry, but which the more prudent usually avoided because of the big mountain of shale which it skirted. That mountain was something like the dynamite which he carried now—passive and safe enough at most times, but always holding a threat of sudden death.

It was not the mountain at which Vick was looking now, however, or even the group of men riding from the west. Instead, he goggled foolishly for a moment at the two horsemen coming from the opposite direction, who would be joining the others in a matter of moments.

Vick's hair seemed to crawl; the coldness was back in him. For these were a pair of nightmare riders, out of a bad dream that he had believed was ended. Two who had come back, it seemed to him, with the smell of brimstone clinging close about them.

It was Calhoun and Shirley who rode there.

21

Vick's first shock lasted only a moment. They were real enough, incredible as it seemed. Bender had reported the house as having collapsed in flaming ruin before he had stopped watching it, and that no one had emerged.

But they had fooled him somehow—probably contriving to get loose and slip out on one side while the cookee watched the other. They were there, alive and unhurt, and now that they were joining the others—men from Window Sash and a few from the town, others from Lone Pine itself —and that last story of dreadful infamy would be told. Vick knew that the jig was up.

An hour before, the notion of running for his very life, as Bender had suggested, had seemed unthinkable. As he had told the cookee, he was a man of property, and you didn't just go off and leave a spread like Wagon Wheel.

Now that attitude seemed almost as foolish to him as the opposite had seemed when the idea was broached. What was money, even a ranch like Wagon Wheel, as compared to your own neck? For as he had seen the others, so had they seen him. And already some of them were starting with the idea of meeting up with him.

It was too late to hope for one last desperate stand with his own crew behind him and an unsuspected and dreadful weapon in his hands to use in turning the scales. Probably his crew, by now, were doing like Bender—running for their lives.

Terror grew in Vick, even as he swung his horse and spurred in a sudden unreasoning fear. But looking back over his shoulder, he saw that there was no chance of getting away. They were swinging now in two groups—some to the right, others to the left. If he kept on as he was going, the main pursuers, heading to take the short-cut around the mountain, would run him down. If he tried to turn and double back, the others would get him.

Calhoun was leading the main chase. There were ten men in it—or nine men and Shirley. For she rode with the others, fully as determined.

Bitterness rose in Vick, a taste like gall in his mouth. By the time they swung past the short-cut, they'd have halved the distance which separated them from him. And then they'd use their guns. He wouldn't even have the satisfaction of being close, to hurl this bomb which he had so carefully contrived, into the middle of a close-packed group and wipe them out—

The idea jerked Vick as savagely as his own hands yanked back on the reins and brought his horse, snorting bloody foam, on to its haunches again. For an instant he sat there, considering his idea, and triumph rose in him again. This was something which couldn't fail; something that would give him the revenge he craved, and turn defeat into victory again.

He looked back, cool and calculating now. It couldn't have been better if he had planned every move in advance and had somehow managed to get them to do as he wished. The main body of his pursuers, the ten, were for the moment out of sight of him, behind the hill. There were just two left in the other bunch, far back now, waiting to cut him off if he tried to double back.

They would be able to see him, of course, and perhaps to guess what was going on. But they were too far off to do anything about it, or to give any warning to the ten. And if they pursued him later, they would be too far behind to be a serious threat.

Vick turned, and spurred up the slope of the big shale mountain. On this side it was not raw and ugly, a thing of loose stone, as on the opposite slope. Here there was a little soil reaching two thirds of the way to the crest, with a thin and tenuous growth of grass, even an occasional bush.

He rode halfway up; then, when the grass grew scanty and the risk of even a horse's hooves great, he dismounted and left his cayuse and went on, carrying his bomb. He reached the crest, panting a little, and saw the others off down below, just about where he had expected them. Triumph made a pleasant taste in his mouth, for Calhoun rode with the others. The man had had a long string of luck, but this time it had run out. Vick raised his arm, like a man about to throw a discus.

Calhoun's emotions were a tangle, as he rode with the others. For the things that he had done, the leadership which he still exercised, they had to get Vick, of course. There was no question about that. But somehow he was not nearly so excited

248

about that as he would have been even a few days before. Nor half so sure of himself and a lot of the things which he had believed then.

He had been very sure of himself, when he had come first to Sage. And of what course a man should take, whatever the situation. A man was a fool not to know his own mind, not to act in his own interest first. It was an easy rule of thumb.

Now he was not sure. There were other values that he had only vaguely sensed before, which had emerged as real and worthwhile. He glanced at Shirley, and she smiled back at him, where she rode beside him.

Somehow, she had taught him a lot of new things that he'd never guessed at before, and beside them, hate, and the ability to hit hard, were not nearly so important as they once had seemed. Nor was a man's own interest always of paramount importance—

He knew, deep down, that he was more lucky than he had ever guessed. He was learning things about values which Vick had never discovered, and never would. He felt sobered and humbly grateful.

And then, for no particular reason, he raised his eyes and saw Vick outlined on the rim of the hill, far above, with something upraised in his hand. And he was shocked back to reality.

Like the others, he had been very certain in his mind that Vick was still fleeing, with the desperation of the hunted. Beholding him up there was staggering. And though he had no notion of what it was that Vick held, Calhoun knew the nature of the hill and realized all too well what he was up to.

Ahead of them now the road was narrowing—to that canyon-like passage which, along with the ever-latent peril of the crouching hill, had made this route impracticable for all except men on horseback, and in so big a hurry that the slight risk always existent here could be discounted. At that point two horsemen might ride together, but only by crowding. It was entirely too narrow for a wagon.

And it was too late to turn back. They had to get through that gap, or be buried here. Calhoun doubted if it could be done, even if there had been only one or two. The potentialities of the great hill of shale were like those of dynamite itself. Get them in action once, and it was a mighty, relentless force.

Now it was starting. They all heard the muffled roar of the dynamite in the bomb and, looking up, were in time to see a vast rolling cloud of dust and shale mushrooming skyward. Out of it was emerg-

ing a new and even greater sound—the movement
of a whole restless hill being jarred out of a taut
lethargy and set in motion.

High above them the slide was gathering mo-
mentum, spreading out like a vast fan, rolling
like a spreading storm. Someone, terrified, drove in
the spurs and his horse bounded ahead. The con-
tagion of fear spread to all of them, but Calhoun's
voice boomed above the thunder, steadying them.

"Only two at a time!" he bellowed. "Don't pile
up or we're all trapped!"

For a moment, he doubted if they had heard
him or would heed. These men were brave enough
in most emergencies, and would face gunfire without flinching. But this mass which was sweeping to
engulf them was something out of their ken; a
thing holding in it all the primeval terrors that
man had known in ages of darkness.

Two or three were not paying any attention.
They were trying to force their horses ahead in a
rush which would have jammed them all tight and
blocked the way hopelessly. But Glades was not one
of them.

Steadying his own horse, which had caught the
rumble and felt the fear running out of the earth
and into the very marrow of its bones, Glades
reached out and grabbed a bridle-rein and jerked

the cayuse back, and took the wild stroke of a quirt on his arm and did not flinch. He knew terror when he saw it in a man.

"One at a time," he growled. "It's our only chance."

Then they were getting through, and Shirley, with an agonized glance at Calhoun, obeyed him and followed the others. Finally Glades accepted the nod of the boss and they thundered through, almost together, with the pile of the mountain poised above.

No need now to urge their horses to greater effort. Here the gap widened, giving them plenty of room—but already the foot of the mountain was shaking with the jar of the slide, the whole thing was spewing and tumbling, its roar drowning out all other sound.

And to pour a mountain and spread part of it out across a flat, like batter-cake on a frying pan, would take all the room in the widening gap—all there was, and more.

The dust hit Calhoun like choking fog, reminding him of chaff near a threshing machine. It blotted out of view even Shirley, just ahead, of the others who rode there. He saw the sliding shale spreading out and enveloping his horse's feet in a slippery, treacherous mass, sensed rather than saw that an overwhelming wave of it was rolling through the dust at them.

Somehow his horse struggled on. Then for a moment it fought free of the stuff. Calhoun knew fresh hope that they might make it, and in that instant it was all about them again. He heard a cry, choked and despairing, and though now night had descended in untimely fashion, saw Shirley, where her horse was down and trapped.

Calhoun did not hesitate. He knew now what he wanted of life, and if this was the end, then he could face it. He jumped from the saddle and left his horse to save itself, and somehow he managed to pull Shirley loose and up to her feet.

"Keep climbing!" he shouted in her ear, and, clutching her arm, did it himself. It seemed hopeless, trying to drag a foot from the clutching, sliding, slippery stuff, to set it higher and repeat the process endlessly. This was dry, yet it was quicksand. The thing was like a nightmare which had no end. They couldn't keep it up much longer, and the wonder was that they had managed to struggle this long.

And then, a little thickly, for his mind was sluggish with weariness, Calhoun realized that the roar was no longer deafening him, that the movement beneath his feet had ceased. They clung to each other and rested, gasping for breath, and gradually the pall lifted a little, and they began unsteadily, with frequent small slides bothering them, to pick their way past the devastation.

Everyone had gotten out, Glades reported, which was something close to a miracle.

"What about Vick?" Calhoun asked.

The two who had stayed back to cut off his retreat had seen it all.

"He started to throw something—dynamite, I guess. Figured he was back far enough to be safe, I reckon. But the slide spread a lot faster than he'd figgered. Caught him and took him right along with it."

"Which," Glades explained, back at the bunk house that evening, "is about what Calhoun did then, with Shirley—picked her up and took her right along with him—and she sure wasn't kickin' none." He kicked off a boot with a thump.

"Looks like a double weddin'," he added, and frowned at Muskett. "Huh? Well, every man to his taste, I guess. All I got to say is—good night!"

www.ingramcontent.com/pod-product-compliance
Lightning Source LLC
Chambersburg PA
CBHW020751250626
47155CB00003B/1017